Within the Storm

A CHRISTIAN ROMANCE
SEASONS OF FAITH BOOK 3

Milla Holt

REINBOK LIMITED
London, United Kingdom

Published by Reinbok Limited, 111 Wolsey Drive, Kingston Upon Thames, Greater London, KT2 5DR

Cover by 100Covers

Within the Storm / Milla Holt. -- 1st ed.

ISBN 978-1-913416-20-1
Print ISBN 978-1-913416-21-8

WELCOME TO THE MOSAIC COLLECTION

WE ARE SISTERS, A beautiful mosaic united by the love of God through the blood of Christ.

Each month The Mosaic Collection releases one or more faith-based novels or anthologies exploring our theme, Family by His Design, and sharing stories that feature diverse, God-designed families. Stories range from mystery and women's fiction to comedic and literary fiction. We hope you'll join our Mosaic family as we explore together what truly defines a family.

If you're like us, loneliness and suffering have touched your life in ways you never imagined; but Dear One, while you may feel alone in your suffering—whatever it is—you are never alone!

Learn more about The Mosaic Collection at
www.mosaiccollectionbooks.com
Join our Reader Community, too!
www.facebook.com/groups/TheMosaicCollection

BOOKS IN THE MOSAIC COLLECTION

When Mountains Sing by Stacy Monson
Unbound by Eleanor Bertin
The Red Journal by Deb Elkink
A Beautiful Mess by Brenda S. Anderson
Hope is Born: A Mosaic Christmas Anthology
More Than Enough by Lorna Seilstad
The Road to Happenstance by Janice L. Dick
This Side of Yesterday by Angela D. Meyer
Lost Down Deep by Sara Davison
The Mischief Thief by Johnnie Alexander
Before Summer's End: Stories to Touch the Soul
Tethered by Eleanor Bertin
Calm Before the Storm by Janice L. Dick
Heart Restoration by Regina Rudd Merrick
Pieces of Granite by Brenda S. Anderson
Watercolors by Lorna Seilstad
A Star Will Rise: A Mosaic Christmas Anthology II
Eye of the Storm by Janice L. Dick
Totally Booked: A Book Lover's Companion

Contents

To my husband and children. You know why.

Chapter One

WHAT WAS IT ABOUT webcams? Bethany Meland angled her laptop screen so her nose wouldn't resemble a bulbous alien growth on her scheduled video call.

She combed her fingers through her dark brown bangs. Few people knew she wore a full wig, but it was a must unless she wanted to expose her bald head to the world. To hide her advanced androgenetic alopecia, she'd gone for a pixie cut with her new made to measure hair piece. She was still getting used to the way the

cropped style accentuated her bone structure.

At least her skin looked good on camera. Her ochre complexion, still dewy in her early forties, was the one feature of which she was proud.

Around her, the newsroom of the *Berghaven Post* was deserted, as it always was on Tuesday mornings. Today's edition of the bi-weekly paper was out, delivered to the doorsteps and corner stores of Berghaven. All around the coastal town in the far north of Norway, people were taking in their paper to enjoy with their morning coffee.

It was the perfect time for Bethany to have an important professional conversation that had nothing to do with her day job.

The call came through at half past seven on the dot, and Pernille Johansen's face filled Bethany's laptop screen.

The editor with Forest House Publishing wasn't smiling, but she rarely did. "Good morning, Bethany. Thanks for making the time to talk to me."

"Not a problem at all," Bethany said. As if she'd not move heaven and earth to schedule this call.

Forest House was publishing her biography of her late husband, Espen. She'd started writing it as a way to work through her grief over his unexpected death five years ago and had been stunned when it became the sub-

ject of a bidding war between three major publishing companies.

Espen Meland was one of Norway's most famous actors and his life had been cut short just as the world was recognizing his extraordinary talent. Bethany wanted her book to cement his legacy.

Forest House had held onto the manuscript for several months. Hopefully the feedback was good.

Pernille adjusted her half-moon glasses. "Before we get into the notes on your book, I have some news."

Bethany held her breath. Pernille's face was impossible to read at the best of times, but through a screen it was impossible to tell what was coming.

Pernille cleared her throat. "Have you heard about Craig Carstone?"

The name rang a bell. A deep, ominous toll. "He's a celebrity biographer, isn't he?"

"Yes. They call him The Undertaker because he buries people's reputations. We have it on good authority that he's working on a biography of your late husband, and his chief source is Annika Elberg."

The tolling bell in Bethany's head took on the tone of a death knell. Annika Elberg was the leggy blond actress who'd played alongside Espen in two of his most successful movies. She'd been present at the boating accident which killed him. Fans and the media hailed him as a hero for saving the lives of Annika and two other passengers, although scandal sheets questioned the nature of his relationship with her.

Bethany never paid attention to the kind of muck raked up by bottom feeder gossip sites. As the wife of a celebrity, she'd soon learned that ignoring the gutter press was the best way to hang on to her sanity. But she couldn't overlook a book by a well-known author.

"Let me guess," she said. "You don't think it's going to be positive?"

Pernille's mouth curved upward, but her smile held no humor. "Judging from his past work, he's probably not nominating your husband for any accolades. The word from upstairs is they want to make sure your book comes out before Carstone's. We suspect his will be published in November. So, yours has to come out in October at the latest. We're bringing your publication date forward."

Bethany's chest felt like a buffalo stampede. She inhaled slowly. "Okay. That should be fine, right, since the manuscript is complete?"

"That brings me to my next point." Pernille brushed a strand of pale blond hair behind her ear. "There are some issues with your manuscript as it stands."

The buffaloes thundered louder. "What issues?"

"Carstone has made a name for himself with controversial biographies.

So, we think your book will need to be more than a sentimental memoir. We want it to have a harder edge to it."

"You think my book is a sentimental memoir?" Heat crept up her neck. "I don't understand what you mean."

Pernille raised her hand. "Hear me out. Your manuscript is great, and we all love it. But it's a bit too rosy a picture of Espen's life. We want more shades of gray if it's to have credibility. Especially when it sits on the shelf alongside Carstone's book."

Bethany pressed her lips tightly together. It sounded as though they wanted her to sling some mud on Espen's name. She forced herself to take three breaths before she spoke. "Okay.

How am I supposed to make the book less rosy?"

"I know this is hard to take, Bethany. Believe me. One of the great things about your book is how you're not just a good writer but Espen's widow. You can bring something really special, which is why the guys upstairs were so keen on the story you have to tell."

Were. In the past tense. They "were keen." Did that mean they weren't anymore?

"Think of it from their point of view," Pernille said. "They're thinking about potential movie options from this book, which is a real possibility. Who do you think Hollywood would approach for source material for an

Espen Meland biopic? I'd love it to be your book and not Carstone's. But Hollywood likes life stories with a bit of grit. We'd love to reach readers beyond Espen's fan base."

Bethany knew she needed to force herself to think clinically about this book. She had to consider it as a publisher and not like a widow writing about the love of her life, whom she'd lost. She bit down on her lip.

Pernille leaned forward. "I'm being frank with you because I want to make sure this book gets published. The guys upstairs are wondering whether you're not too close to this project. So, I have to ask you. Can you do it? Can you make the changes we need?"

Bethany sighed. "Okay. What kinds of changes do they want?"

"It's all in the notes I'm going to send you. But for one thing, your manuscript is a bit thin on what Espen's life was like before he was a movie star. We'd love more on how he got his start. What was his childhood like? Who was Espen Meland the boy, the man, before he became Espen Meland, the A-list actor? You're uniquely placed to tell that part of his story. Carstone can't do that. And don't be afraid to make the narrative more nuanced. No one gets to Espen's level of success without stepping on a few toes, or without being a driven, maybe even obsessive person. We'd love to see more of that side of things, if it's there."

The key word was if. "And what will happen if I can't find any gritty stuff on him?"

Pernille stared over the rims of her glasses. "Try. Try hard. I'll be frank with you, Bethany. I've seen projects pulled when they were already well down the pipeline for publication. If the guys upstairs think the manuscript can't compete with Carstone's, they'll shelve it. Perhaps permanently. And right now, there are serious questions."

Bethany clenched her fists in her lap. So, because of a guy who made his living trashing the reputation of people more successful than himself, she had to go looking for dirt on her husband. But what choice did she have? Pernille was a straight shooter. She'd never have told Bethany all this if it weren't true.

Bethany gritted her teeth. "Okay. I'll do everything I can."

"Excellent. I'll send you my notes. Do you think you could deliver a revised manuscript within the next two months?"

"Just two months? That'll be tight."

"I know," Pernille said. "But it has to be if we're to get it out in English and Norwegian and produce the audiobook for release alongside the hardbacks. So, will you do it?"

Bethany did a mental run through her commitments. To deliver the level of revisions Pernille wanted, she'd have to cancel her plans for the summer. If she didn't do it, Carstone's hatchet job would come out before her book. There was no other option. She had to meet that deadline. Somehow.

Sending a silent SOS heavenward, she looked into her web cam. "Okay. I'll do it."

Chapter Two

The second the clock hit two that afternoon, Bethany called her best friend and sister-in-law Lisa.

Lisa's husband Kai, a successful thriller author, was a guest lecturer at a semester-long creative writing course in Missouri, and he'd taken his family with him. It was seven in the morning there, so Lisa would surely be up by now feeding their six-month-old baby.

Lisa answered within seconds, an early morning rasp in her voice. "Hey,

Bethany. Is there anything wrong? Is it Eline?"

Bethany smiled into the phone. Lisa's thoughts always flew to her eldest child, even though Eline was now a grown woman settled into a happy marriage of her own. "Eline is all right, as far as I know. Everyone's okay."

"Good." Lisa let out a puff of air. "Then why on earth are you calling me at this hour?"

"I'm sorry; did I wake you up?"

"No, I was already awake. I just finished settling Bella down. So, what's going on?"

"I wouldn't have bothered you out of the blue with an early morning call unless it was important. It's about the book I'm writing about Espen."

"What about it?"

Bethany filled her in on what the editor had said, finishing with, "I need more background material on Espen from the time before I met him. Childhood things and information about when he was just getting into acting. I thought maybe Kai could help?"

"I'll ask him for you," Lisa said. "Give me a second. I think I heard him getting up."

Kai yawned on the other side of the phone. "Hey, Beth. Lisa says you need info about Espen?"

"Hi. Yes, I do. My publisher is asking for more information and anecdotes from his early life, so I need to interview people who knew him. You, for example. You could tell me things about what he was like as a child, your home life, the environment you all grew up in. And some photos from back then would really help, too."

"I can tell you some things, of course, but I'm not sure I'm the best person to talk to. Espen and I weren't that close, and I was wrapped up with my own friends and extra-curricular stuff." Kai paused for a moment. "Your best bet would be to talk to Lukas. He's older, so he would remember things about our home growing up that I've either forgotten or that passed over my head."

Bethany winced. She'd been afraid Kai would suggest she speak to his eldest brother Lukas.

"He and Espen were very close when we were younger," Kai said. "I was the third wheel. The two of them used to hang out with the same drama and theater crowd. He could tell you a lot more about how Espen got his early break and who his friends were. And if there are any family photos, he's got those, too. I think he has all of Mama's stuff, and that would include albums and keepsakes and those sorts of things."

Bethany stifled a sigh. "That's really helpful. Thanks. I'd still like to talk through anything you remember, though. I know you've probably got to get ready for work, but maybe we could set up a time?"

"Of course. Saturday mornings would be best. Any time from, say, nine o'clock over here. That would be, what, four Norwegian time?"

"Sounds good. I'll call this weekend."

"Good stuff. Do you still need to talk to Lisa? I'll hand the phone over."

Lisa came back on the line. "Sounds like Kai's pointed you in the right direction."

"Yes." Bethany kept her voice neutral. "He thinks Lukas is the best person to talk to."

"That makes sense."

"On paper. But do you think he'll talk to me?"

"Why wouldn't he?" Lisa asked.

Bethany hesitated, unsure how to put her thoughts into words. "I don't know. He just seems to clam up whenever I enter the room, although he doesn't have any trouble talking to other people. And..."

"And what?" Lisa asked, filling in the silence after Bethany's sentence trailed off.

"No, nothing, really. That was a long time ago." Bethany shook her head.

"What? Now you've really got me curious."

Bethany sighed. "Espen told me Lukas refused to be his best man. He said Lukas didn't want him to marry me."

"What?" The shock in Lisa's voice carried across an ocean and into

Bethany's ear. "Are you sure about that?"

"It's what Espen said. So, along with that and the way he just acts so reserved around me, I'm not all that comfortable asking him to do me a favor like this."

"Wow. That's news to me. Would you like me or Kai to talk to him so at least you can get the stuff you need for your book?"

Bethany hesitated. The idea was tempting. Get Kai to ask Lukas for contacts she could approach for background material on Espen. But, no, she needed to act like a grown woman. "Thanks for the offer, but I think I'd better speak to him myself. I don't want things to be more awkward than they need to be."

"Okay, if you're sure. But for the record, whatever Espen said, I'd have sworn that Lukas—" An infant wailed in the background. "Oh dear, sounds like Bella's up again. I've got to go."

"I won't keep you," Bethany said. "Thanks so much for your help, and sorry for rousting you out of bed."

Lisa laughed. "No problem. Speak to you soon."

Bethany ended the call and put the phone on her desk. Whatever she felt about Lukas, he was the best shot she had at getting the material she needed to revise her manuscript. She checked the time. It was almost three. Should she call and make an appointment?

No, that would just drag out the discomfort and anxiety even longer.

She grabbed her purse and stood. Things were still quiet in the newsroom, and no one would miss her if she slipped out for an hour. She'd better talk to Lukas and get it over with. Then if he turned her down, she'd know straight away and formulate Plan B.

Chapter Three

LUKAS MELAND STARED AT his PA, Greta, and didn't like what he saw in her face. It was bad enough that his body was failing him. He didn't want to be the object of anyone's pity.

A crease deepened between her eyebrows and she smoothed the gray hair in her sleek bun. "I meant it, Lukas. I can postpone my relocation for a few weeks. Just until you get over this hump."

He shook his head. "That's not an option. Didn't you tell me you've already sold your home and are ready to move? Besides, I accepted your resignation months ago, and your grandson's due date is almost here. Your family needs you. I'll manage."

"Really?" She looked around the document-strewn desk in his home office. "It was really unprofessional of that new PA to quit so suddenly. Maybe I should have trained her better. At least then you wouldn't be in such a pinch."

Lukas gathered a handful of papers. "It's not your fault Ingrid couldn't keep up. You've been doing the work of two executive assistants, so I should have known I'd need more than one person to replace you. Seriously, though. I'll be fine."

He wasn't sure whether he was trying to convince Greta or himself. She knew his work affairs as well as he did. And she was well aware that his business was in its worst crisis since she'd come on board twenty years ago.

When Lukas became unwell in early spring, he'd soldiered on, thinking he was just a bit rundown. But a week ago he'd woken up to find the left side of his face was paralyzed. After his initial panic that he was having a stroke, the ER doctors had assured him that wasn't the case. Lab tests showed he had Lyme disease, which had triggered the freezing of his facial muscles.

He wasn't going to die just yet—probably—but standing in front of people giving seminars and hands-on coaching was his bread and butter as a productivity coach. Even if he could have pushed his body to fight against the bone deep fatigue and muscle pain, he couldn't inspire confidence with half his face frozen.

He needed someone to fill in for him on a couple of training contracts for important clients. And that was besides hiring a replacement for the PA who had quit without notice. Greta's resignation had been planned months ago, before he fell ill, and he didn't want to disrupt her relocation to her family.

Greta rested her hands on her hips. "I'll see whether the recruitment bureau has sent any messages about a temp. Even if all they can do is answer phones and sort mail, that'll be something."

"Thanks. And I'll keep trying to get a hold of Gunnar."

Lukas turned to his phone. His friend and fellow management consultant Gunnar Rikardson would be the ideal replacement to run the training sessions Lukas couldn't fulfill. If Gunnar couldn't do it, Lukas would have to postpone or cancel the contract and take the consequences. He'd rather do that than hand the contract over to a consultant he didn't trust.

As he dialed Gunnar's number, Lukas watched Greta move around her office. She was only a decade older than he was, and equally dedicated to

her work. But, unlike him, she had a life beyond the office. She was moving several hundred miles south to be closer to her daughter and grandchild. Although her husband was gone now, she had the next generations to nurture. Lukas had nothing, a fact his illness had made all too painfully clear. His focus was building his career. But when he couldn't work, what did he have left?

He cleared his throat as his call went to voicemail. "Hey, Gunnar. It's Lukas. Call me as soon as you can. Speak to you soon."

He put down the phone, exhaustion washing over his body like a brutal wave. *Lord, I could use some help.*

The doorbell rang. Thank God Greta was still here to deal with it. If he'd been on his own, he'd have ignored whoever it was. Probably someone delivering a package.

Right now, he just wanted to go upstairs and lie down for a few minutes before trying Gunnar again, and figuring out what to do with his podcast, blog posts and other content channels.

The doctor said the antibiotics should clear out the Lyme infection within a few weeks, but she'd emphasized that Lukas needed to rest in order to give his body the best chance to heal. They'd caught the disease in its early disseminated phase, but if they failed to deal with it, it might progress to further long-term complications, involving joint pain, heart rhythm ir-regularities, and problems with his concentration and short-term memory.

Lukas didn't even want to consider what that would mean for his business or his life. Hopefully, the treatment would work and he'd get better while he still had a business to save.

Greta came back into his office, her face clouded. "There's someone here to see you, but I wasn't sure whether to tell her you're in. She says she's your sister-in-law."

His sister-in-law? Lisa was in Amer-ica with Kai. That could only mean—

"Shall I send her in?" Greta asked.

What could Bethany want? Lukas's fingers went up to the left side of his face, the side frozen and drooping as though someone had held a candle too close to a wax figure. He didn't want Bethany to see him like this. And yet she must need something, or she wouldn't have come here.

His gaze met Greta's, and he nodded. "Yes, please send her in."

Chapter Four

ETHANY WAITED IN THE living room for the gray-haired woman to come back.

Lukas ran his business from home. Perhaps that was why, although the decor was tasteful, it had a sterile feel. Kai and Lisa's cabin had family pictures on the walls and hand-braided rugs on the floors. Espen had liked larger-than-life portraits of himself to dominate the accent walls in their home.

But Lukas's living room, while impeccable, told her nothing about the man who lived and worked here. Apart from a Bible on the mantel. She and Lukas were members of the same church, but seldom spoke.

Lisa and her believing friends had had a long talk with Bethany about being "unequally yoked" when she'd married Espen. At the time, she'd been convinced it didn't matter that Espen wasn't a professing Christian.

Both his brothers were Christians, and Espen had mocked their faith, calling it a helpful crutch for weak people and a good excuse for others to feel morally superior. Kai, for all his faith, had shipwrecked his marriage with his gambling addiction. And

Lukas, whom Espen had called a "pillar of rectitude," was cold and aloof.

Espen never clarified which camp he thought Bethany fit into—weak or Pharisaical.

Lukas's secretary came back. "Mr. Meland will see you now. Come this way, please."

Bethany followed her down the hallway, catching a fleeting glimpse of a large kitchen on the left and a well-stocked library on the right.

Bethany went into the room the secretary indicated, stopping short as her gaze landed on Lukas.

It had been a few weeks since she'd seen him. What had happened? He was pale and gaunt, and something was wrong with his face. Had he had a stroke? Surely, Kai or Lisa would have mentioned it.

"Well, this is unexpected," he said. His voice was unnervingly like Espen's. "Please have a seat. What can I do for you?"

Staring at his strangely lopsided mouth, she lowered herself onto the edge of the chair he indicated. The threads of her prepared speech scattered like wayward balls of yarn.

A phone rang in the next room, jarring the silence.

"It's Bell's Palsy," he said.

"I'm sorry, what?"

"The facial paralysis. It's Bell's Palsy."

Her cheeks warmed as she dragged her gaze away from his face. "I'm... I'm sorry. I didn't know you were unwell. Is it serious? I don't know anything about Bell's Palsy."

He shrugged. "It's a complication of Lyme disease. The doctor says it should clear up within a few weeks."

Lyme disease. That was something she *had* heard about. "I see. Now I'm really sorry for just turning up without phoning first. Is this a bad time?"

"Perhaps not the best, but you're here now."

It wasn't exactly a resounding welcome, but she'd take it. Lukas always kept her at arm's length, so his cool response was normal.

She cleared her throat. "I'll make it quick. You're probably not aware that I'm writing Espen's biography."

His right eyebrow went up. "No, I wasn't aware of that."

"I've got most of it written, and Forest Tree Publishing wants to publish it later this year. But they got back to me today wanting significant revisions. My editor says it needs more—"

The door opened behind her, and Lukas's secretary spoke. "I'm sorry to interrupt you, Mr. Meland, but I thought you might want to take this call. It's from Gunnar Rikardson."

Lukas straightened up in his seat. "Send it through, please." He turned to Bethany as his secretary left the room. "Sorry, I've been waiting for this call all day."

He picked up the handset as soon as the phone on his desk rang, before

Bethany could ask whether he'd like her to step out of his office.

"Hey, Gunnar. Thanks for getting back to me. You've read my email? Yeah, no, you've got to just roll with the punches, right?"

He listened for a moment, his face breaking into half a grin. His smile, askew though it was, transformed his face. It gave a glimpse of the friendly side Lisa and Kai swore he had.

Bethany couldn't remember the last time he'd smiled at her.

He spoke into the phone again. "You're a lifesaver. I seriously owe you. You have no idea. Thank you so much. I'll give you access to the shared drive with all the files and background info you need."

Bethany wondered who Lukas was speaking to. It must be someone he was close to. She knew so little about him. As far as she knew, he wasn't dating anyone. He must be almost fifty years old. Why hadn't he ever gotten married?

He laughed, a warm, rich sound. "Brilliant. I'll send you an email with the access code. I've got to go now—someone's waiting to speak to me. But can I call you back in about an hour? Excellent. Speak to you soon."

He put the phone down and looked across his desk at Bethany. "Bear with me for a moment while I take care of something."

Bethany fiddled with the strap of her purse while Lukas's fingers moved across his keyboard. His hands were much like Espen's. But where Espen's were smooth and pampered—he never missed his weekly paraffin manicure—Lukas's were sinewy, the veins prominent, his nails short and blunt.

He turned to face her, clicking his mouse button. "That's done. So, you were saying you're writing a book?"

The doorbell sounded as she answered him. "Yes. A biography of Espen. My publisher would like it to include more anecdotes from his early years, and they're especially keen to know more about his family background and how he first became interested in acting. They also want pictures from when he was younger. I already spoke to Kai, but he said he doesn't have any photos from back then. He thought maybe you might have some of the family albums."

"Sorry to bother you, Mr. Meland." The secretary spoke from the doorway. "There's a young lady here to interview for the PA role. I had no idea she was coming. The recruitment bureau sent her, but their message to me must have landed in my spam box. Anyway, she's here."

Half of Lukas's face registered surprise, which only emphasized the waxen stillness of the other side of his face. "That was quick. As long as she has a pulse and can answer a phone, we'll probably hire her. Hopefully she'll be able to start ASAP. Could you run her through your most basic duties and get a feel for what kind of experience she has to handle those? I'll join you in the dining room in a few minutes."

He turned back to Bethany. "You were saying you want baby pictures of Espen?"

She opened her mouth to answer, but a cellphone on his desk rang.

He glanced at the screen. "I need to speak to this gentleman."

Her face heated up. Lukas was unwell with his frozen face Lyme disease thing, and there seemed to be some situation going on here. And she'd just barged in, looking as though all she wanted were some trivial mementos of her husband.

Bethany's heart sank. She should never have shown up here. She was little more than a nuisance.

Chapter Five

As Lukas answered his phone, he slammed on his mental armor, falling into a decades-long habit of guarding his heart against the woman who sat opposite him.

Of course, it was about Espen. It always was. It shouldn't surprise him that his brother was the only reason Bethany was reaching out to him.

He wrestled his mind to focus on his client, the human resources executive at the other end of the phone line. "One of my closest associates has confirmed that he will take over the training weekend. I can vouch for his skills and qualifications, and I'm sure he'll be an excellent replacement for me. In fact, don't tell him I said so, but although I developed the training materials, I think his presentation skills are far better than mine."

"That's good to know," Mr. Erlandsen said. "With changes at such short notice, and with the resources we've dedicated to this training package, I'm sure you can understand why my associates are so anxious."

"I understand completely," Lukas said.

He hated last-minute changes as much as Mr. Erlandsen's associates. Unfortunately, getting ill and being unable to fulfill his training engagements wasn't something Lukas could schedule ahead of time.

Even now, fatigue rolled in from the edges of his mind like a creeping fog. His body screamed for rest. But he understood the HR man's need for reassurance. "I'll send my training colleague's resume to you within the hour so you can assure your associates that he is fully qualified to lead the session. If there's anything else I can do for you, please let me know."

As he ended the call, his gaze met Bethany's. She sat upright, her fingers curled around her purse strap. She still wore her platinum wedding ring. What had his brother done to deserve the devotion of a woman like this?

He glanced at his watch. The PA candidate was waiting to be interviewed, but he wanted to finish this business with Bethany. "You were saying you need pictures from when Espen was young, right?"

She nodded. "Yes, but it's not just baby pictures. My publisher wants more about who Espen was before he became famous. What kind of childhood he had, how he got interested in acting, what led up to his first big break. I wouldn't have bothered you and I approached Kai first, but he said he and Espen weren't close, so he'll not be able to tell me much."

That made sense. Kai was wrapped up in his own interests when the boys were younger. "When do you need this information?"

"As soon as possible. My publisher has moved up the deadline because there's another biography of Espen coming out this year."

He shot her a glance. "Oh?"

"Yes." She shifted in her seat. "And judging from the people involved in writing it, this other biography will probably lean toward a negative, sensationalist account of Espen's life and career."

Lukas nodded slowly. So, that's what was going on. Someone was writing a book that might tarnish the image of the golden boy Espen Meland, Norway's greatest export besides petroleum products and fish. "When will your book come out?"

"Hopefully in October. They think the other book is releasing in November."

Lukas crossed his arms. It wasn't a surprise that Bethany and her publishers would want her book to come out first. Although the critical and sensationalist book might well paint a more accurate picture of his brother.

He loved Espen, but was under no illusions about his multi-talented brother's deep flaws and some of the unethical things he'd done. Some of it had directly impacted Bethany. If she knew even half of what Lukas knew, she wouldn't be here wanting to rush out her book about her husband.

"What exactly do you want from me?" he asked.

Her shoulders relaxed. "Pictures, like we said, of when he was younger, and any mementos or keepsakes that would help me flesh out that part of his life. And if you know of anyone who knew him in his childhood or teen years who would talk to me, that would be great. It would be even better if they were involved in his early acting efforts. Kai will tell me what he can about your parents and family background."

"Okay," Lukas said slowly. "Any pictures and keepsakes are probably at my place. Mama used to keep them, but when she died and we cleared out her house, all of that sort of thing went straight into my attic. It's been about fifteen years and I don't think anyone's ever sorted through it. We just put the boxes wherever we found space. I could look through it, but it'll take time." Time and energy, neither of which he had. But the smile Bethany beamed at him would spur him beyond the point of exhaustion.

"Thanks. I appreciate that," she said.

Lukas looked away from her face. Finding mementos among the haphazardly stored boxes in his attic was challenging enough. But convincing people who knew Espen from back then to speak to Bethany would be a trickier prospect.

He stroked his chin. "I've not been in touch with the people Espen used to hang out with for quite some time. But I'll make some calls and see who might give you an interview. I'm not promising anything, though. It's been a while."

And Espen had burned many bridges. Should he tell Bethany that? She might very well find out on her own, and he didn't want to be responsible for her pain when it happened. Maybe he ought to give her a heads-up.

Interrupting her thanks, he said, "I may not find anyone who can help you. Like I said, these are people Espen hasn't seen for a long time. Not since he got his big break. And sometimes when a person gets a break like that, their old friends may feel like they've been left behind."

"I understand. But I appreciate your willingness to try."

He pushed his chair back and stood. "I need to leave now, but I'll get back to you when I have anything to report."

She got up, showing him that smile again. "Thanks so much for your time and your help. And I hope you'll get better soon." She walked out of the office.

He should have gone straight to interview the new PA, but he sank back in his chair. He didn't have the mental or physical resources to find the mementos Bethany wanted or to chase down Espen's former associates. But her heart was clearly set on writing this book. For reasons he couldn't fathom, she wanted to honor his brother in this way.

His thoughts flew to another Meland woman who'd been blindly devoted to Espen. Their mother would have wanted this book to come out. Berit Meland had thought the sun rose and set on her youngest son. She'd been so proud of his achievements. Lukas couldn't blame her. Espen had been a bright spot in their mother's life when so many other painful things were going on.

For her sake, he'd do what he could to help Bethany with her project. Even though Espen probably didn't deserve it.

Chapter Six

THE NEXT DAY AT lunchtime, Bethany hustled into a coffee shop around the corner from the *Berghaven Post*.

Thankfully, her brother's wife, Tina, had agreed to meet her here rather than somewhere on the other side of town. Berghaven wasn't big, but Bethany's lunch break was short.

Spring came late this far north of the Arctic Circle. While in Norway's southern cities some cafes were probably already using their outdoor tables, all the Java Bean's customers still crowded inside.

Bethany scanned the crowd, spotting her sister-in-law in a corner booth.

Tina's honey blond hair was freshly highlighted, cut, and blow dried, and her manicured hands held an outsized cup of peppermint tea. Several shopping bags stood next to her feet. Her collagen-thickened lips tilted upward as Bethany approached her table.

"Hi, sweetheart," Tina said, half rising to bestow air kisses on the space next to Bethany's face. "You were a bit late, so I already ordered myself a cup of tea. I'm absolutely rushed off my feet today."

Tina didn't have a job and her young children were both in school. A cleaning lady handled a good deal of the family's chores and an au pair nannied the children, so Bethany wasn't sure what Tina was rushing around doing.

Bethany settled into a chair. "Sorry I'm late. I'm insanely busy, which is why I needed to see you today. I have a favor to ask you about Mama's party."

Tina raised a highly plucked eyebrow. "I'm listening."

"I'll just grab my list." Bethany reached into her purse and pulled out her planner.

Flipping through several pages, she found the one she wanted and ran a finger down the handwritten list. "I've got the caterers and entertainment booked. I was supposed to sign off on the menu, book the venue, and arrange the decorations. But then yesterday my editor got back to me with a ton of extra revisions to make on my manuscript. It'll mean I have a lot less time to spend organizing this party. So, could you take on some of the planning tasks?"

Tina waved her hands before Bethany stopped speaking. "Wait, what? I don't have time to take on any extra work, either. You're not a mother, so perhaps you don't understand, but this is a full-time job."

Bethany didn't want to make any assumptions about what was involved in caring for young children. But it seemed to her that her sister-in-law found plenty of time for her shopping trips and beauty treatments. Maybe that was all part of the self-care mothers needed in order to restore their energy. "I wouldn't ask unless I had to. I really am in a pinch."

Tina shrugged. "Well, I'm in a pinch every day. It's a real squeeze trying to fit everything in. You have no idea what it's like."

Bethany did not. She looked at her planner. "I simply don't have the hours to do all this. I'm taking time off work to finish my book, but even then it's going to be tough to meet my new deadline."

Rolling her eyes, Tina held her hand out for the planner. "Fine. Let me see what's on your list." She pulled the book toward her and scanned the page. "I see you haven't got the venue ticked off yet."

"Not yet, no," Bethany said. "The Garden Table says they'll take us if we confirm and make a deposit within the next forty-eight hours. Would you call and make the reservations? We're expecting forty guests. Maybe allow room for fifty, just in case. Please check whether they allow outside catering—I forgot to ask. And if they don't, then there are two other places you can try. But it needs to be tomorrow at the very latest."

Tina heaved the sigh of a martyr. "Okay, I'll do that."

"Thanks. I'll text you the contact details. The sooner we pin down the venue, the better." Bethany typed on her phone, copying the information from her planner. "Done. Thanks."

"You're welcome," Tina said as her message tone chimed.

Bethany slipped her phone back in her purse.

Only one task was offloaded from her massive to-do list, but that was better than nothing. She could have asked her brother Erik, Tina's husband, to help with the party organization. Astrid was his mother, after all. But Bethany might as well howl into the wind for all the good that would do.

Erik was trying to make it as an app developer and inventor. Although their mother backed several of his business startups, nothing seemed to come to fruition. The market turned, or the economy hit a downturn, or he couldn't compete with cheap supplies or labor from developing countries. Erik's reasons seemed endless.

And, like his wife, he claimed to be too busy to deal with mundane things. The responsibility of organizing their mother's seventy-fifth birthday cele-bration lay squarely on Bethany's shoulders.

A twinge in her stomach reminded her how long it had been since the bowl of muesli she'd grabbed at break-fast, and the blueberry muffins under a glass display made her mouth water. But the idea of staying here and making small talk with Tina did not appeal. She'd get a sandwich from the convenience store instead.

She stood. "I'd better get back to the office. Would you let me know which venue you nail down? Then I'll handle the rest."

"Yes, of course." Tina fiddled with her phone. Probably taking an Instagram worthy snapshot of the salad a waitress set in front of her. "Speak to you soon."

Bethany headed toward the door. With the grand total of one task off her lengthy to do list, she would need to burn the candle at both ends to get this party organized and work on her manuscript.

Chapter Seven

LUKAS STARED AT THE writing on his notepad, the result of twenty minutes' worth of scouring his brain. Did it count as a list when there were only three names?

Of all the people he and Espen had known in their theater group, these three were the only prospects who might give Bethany an interview. And even they were doubtful. Still, he wouldn't know for sure unless he called them. He'd do that after lunch.

He set the notepad on the kitchen counter and pulled open the fridge, wrinkling his nose at the Spartan contents. A couple of protein shakes, ancient cheese, and a handful of rubbery carrots that were sprouting white hairs. He could call for a takeout meal, but the thought of all his usual options turned his stomach. Whether it was because of the Lyme disease or his medication, nothing tasted good anymore.

He pulled out a chocolate-flavored protein shake. It touted itself as a nutritionally complete meal in a bottle. That would have to do. But he'd better stock up on groceries soon. His associate Gunnar Rikardson was coming next week so they could put their heads together and figure out how Gunnar could lighten Lukas's client load while he recovered.

He went into his office, now under control thanks to the new PA. She was no Greta, but over the past few days, she'd done well.

He breathed a prayer of thanks as he settled at his desk. With a competent PA and Gunnar's help, he finally felt his business would remain on an even keel. Maybe God would also help him with Bethany's project.

He dialed the first number on his list.

A man's voice answered. "Hello, Kjell Moen here. Who's this?"

"Hey, Kjell. It's Lukas Meland. It's been a while. How are you?"

Lukas measured the seconds before Kjell spoke again.

"This is unexpected. What can I do for you?"

Lukas cleared his throat. "I won't take up much of your time. I'm calling on behalf of my sister-in-law. Espen's widow. She's writing his biography for Tree House Publishing and wants to speak to people who knew Espen when he was just getting into acting. I wondered whether you'd be willing to speak to her and answer some questions."

Kjell's laugh sounded more like a sharp bark. "Reminisce about the good old days, you mean? I've got to hand it to you, Lukas, you never lacked nerve. But, no. Nothing against you personally, nor against your sister-in-law. I'm sure I don't need to elaborate on why."

Lukas's heart plummeted. "Fair enough. I'm sorry to have bothered you."

"You know, I might have considered it at one time," Kjell said. "When he died, I thought perhaps it was time to let bygones be bygones. I even tried to attend his funeral. But apparently only A-listers were allowed to go. We small folk were turned away."

Lukas winced. "That's very unfortunate. I wish I'd known you were coming. The family trusted Espen's agents to handle the logistics around the funeral because it was such a chaotic time. I had no idea they stopped old friends from coming."

"Yes, well, it reminded me of where we all stand. So, no. I hope you understand."

"Off course. Thanks for being up-front, and all the best."

Lukas hung up the phone and drew a thick black line across Kjell's name. That had gone about as well as could be expected.

He dialed the next number on the list.

A woman answered on the first ring. "Hello?"

"Hello. This is Lukas Meland, Espen Meland's brother. I—"

"No. Don't call this number again."

Lukas stared at his hand set. He knew that Espen had burned his bridges when he moved away to become an actor, but this was ridiculous.

Lukas crossed the second name off his list. Just one person remained.

He dialed the number.

A woman's voice, husky with a smoker's rasp, answered. "Anita Ilseth."

"Hello, Anita. This is Lukas Meland."

"Wow, there's a blast from the past. How are you doing?"

"Reasonably well," Lukas said. "How about you?"

"Can't complain. So, what's going on? To what do I owe the pleasure of this call?"

Lukas clenched a fist. Her voice dripped with sarcasm, but at least she hadn't hung up on him. "I'm calling on behalf of my brother Espen's widow. She's writing his biography and would appreciate some input from people who knew him back in the old days. Before Hollywood came knocking. I know it's a bit of a stretch, but I wondered whether you'd be willing to speak to her."

"His wife is writing his biography, you said? Who else is going to be in it?"

Lukas rubbed his chin. "I'm not sure who else is involved."

"I don't know, Lukas. You know what went down back then. I'm over it and I've made a decent life for myself, but I don't exactly have the warm fuzzies for Espen. Are you sure I'm the right person to speak to?"

"I'll be frank with you. At the moment, you're the only person from back then who's even stayed this long with me on the phone."

Anita laughed. "I'm shocked. Shocked, I tell you. So, none of the old gang are lining up to help. Why is she trying to talk to any of us? Doesn't she want the book to be a puff piece for his legions of fans?"

Lukas hesitated. Bethany might not want her editor's comments shared with people she didn't know, especially someone hostile to Espen. He weighed his words. "She's trying to share his story in a balanced and nu-

anced way, and give space to people who knew Espen even when he wasn't at his best."

"I see. That sounds reasonable. How on earth did Espen get a sensible person like her to marry him with all the groupies swarming around him?" Anita was silent for a second. "You know what? You've made me curious. I'll talk to her, as long as she's prepared to hear things she may not want to. What I say may not be complimentary.

Lukas mouthed a silent prayer of gratitude. He'd fulfilled his obligation, and the rest would be in Bethany's hands. "That's wonderful, Anita. Thanks. Shall I pass on your details to my sister-in-law?"

"Yes. Tell her I'll be waiting for her call."

Chapter Eight

ETHANY'S STOMACH COILED INTO a hard knot as she stepped onto the front porch and raised a hand to the door knocker. She'd done countless interviews in the course of her job. Talking to Anita Ilseth would be no different.

Who was she kidding? She pulled her hand away from the door and wiped her clammy palm on the side of her pant leg, praying God would help her get the information she needed from Anita without blundering.

Forcing herself to breathe slowly, she took in her surroundings. Anita lived in a large single-family home in Halvdal, the town across the fjord from Berghaven. Espen and his brothers had spent their teen years here before he'd moved south to begin his acting career.

She tapped on the knocker before her nervousness grew any more.

The door swung open, and Bethany looked up at a statuesque blonde whose classically beautiful features were enhanced with impeccable makeup.

"Bethany, I presume." Anita's blue gaze swept over Bethany. "You're prettier than in your pictures. I looked you up, of course. Come in."

Anita led the way down a long hall-way, past a blur of contemporary paintings and dazzling light fixtures.

Walking across the living room, Anita gestured to the French doors that opened out onto an expansive ve-randa. "It's such a nice day. I thought we could sit outside. First time I'm able to do that this year. Can I offer you anything? Coffee? Tea?"

Bethany stepped outside. "Coffee would be great, thanks. You have a wonderful view here."

Anita smiled, glancing at the wide mountain panorama. "We bought the view and built the house so we could look at it."

"It's stunning. You're blessed to live here."

Anita quirked an eyebrow. "Why, thank you. That's quite a compliment coming from someone who I imagine has the means to live wherever she wants."

Bethany's cheeks warmed. Espen had left her very well off, but the trappings of his celebrity lifestyle had never felt natural to her. After he died, it had never occurred to her to live anywhere else than in a modest house in her hometown, and her lifestyle matched what she earned as a small town journalist.

Anita went back inside, and Bethany pulled her notebook and voice recorder out of her tote bag. She stared at her list of questions.

Before writing her manuscript, she'd interviewed dozens of people. They all gushed about Espen. His agent, his publicist, heavyweight directors and screenwriters spoke at length about how, with several blockbusters under his belt, Espen was finally getting taken seriously by the critics after a couple of indie roles.

But speaking to Anita was different. She knew an Espen Bethany didn't. Anita's Espen was in his teens, hungry for success, about to break into his first significant role. And her Espen had done something to thoroughly burn his bridges.

Anita walked onto the veranda with a large tray and a silver coffee service. "How do you take your coffee?"

"Milk with no sugar, please."

Bethany pulled the exquisite cup toward her. "Thank you."

"You're not the type of woman I expected Espen to marry, and to stay married to for so long. We were all surprised when we saw the pictures of his wedding. No offense, but I never thought he'd marry a Black girl. He normally went after tall, leggy blondes." She tilted her head. "Like me."

Bethany's head jolted upward.

The other woman laughed. "You look shocked. Didn't your brother-in-law tell you Espen and I used to date?"

"No, he didn't." Heat flooded Bethany's face.

"That was a long time ago, though. A very long time ago. We were just kids. What is it, twenty-five odd years?" Her eyes widened. "Oh my goodness, no. It's more like thirty years. I can't believe how old I'm getting. Anyway, what can I tell you? Lukas said you want me to reminisce about the time I knew Espen."

"Yes." Bethany pointed to her recorder. "Do you mind if I tape our conversation? It'll allow me to concentrate more on talking with you rather than being distracted by taking notes."

Anita pursed her lips. "What will happen to the recording?"

"I'll get the interview transcribed and the recording will be destroyed.

No one but me and the transcriptionists will have access to it, and they're bound by a strict confidentiality agreement, if that's what you're worried about."

Anita shrugged. "If confidentiality was an issue, I wouldn't be speaking to you. I was just curious about how these things are handled." She glanced at her watch. "I have about an hour until I need to collect my daughter from school. What do you want to know?"

"I'd like to know how you and Espen met. What was the sort of crowd you used to hang out in?"

"I've known him since junior high when his family moved over here. He was cute and everyone took notice of him. At the time, though, the girls used to swoon over his oldest brother. Lukas is the one who really got the community theater going. He put in hours and hours getting the group off the ground."

Anita's lips curved upward and her eyes softened. "We worked so hard on those productions. But it was fun. We did Shakespeare, Ibsen, even attempted some Gilbert and Sullivan. But Lukas was the star."

Bethany stared at her. "Lukas?"

Anita's gaze snapped back to Bethany's face. "Yes, Lukas. He was hands down the best actor. I was just a clueless kid, but I and everyone else agreed that Lukas became whatever character he played."

Interesting. But Bethany wasn't here to talk about Lukas. "When did Espen get involved with the group?"

"Oh, yes, Espen. He fell into the group by accident. We were doing the *Merchant of Venice*. The man playing Bassanio broke his leg in a skiing accident two days before opening night, and Lukas asked Espen to step in."

Anita took a sip of coffee. "We were all so nervous. Word had gone out that a casting agent from Oslo was coming all the way to our little town to watch the performance. We all thought the agent was here because Lukas had made such a name for himself over the past months.

"Opening night came, and we crushed that play. I was Jessica and

Lukas played Shylock. But Espen stole every scene he appeared in. In the end, the casting agent wanted to talk to him, and no one else. Not even Lukas."

Bethany exhaled a sharp breath. So, Lukas was the star and Espen stole his spotlight. That must have stung.

Anita turned her gaze to Bethany. "We were all happy for Espen, of course. It was so exciting that one of us had a living, breathing agent. And if he found success, that meant there was a chance for the rest of us, right? The agent had a role in mind for him, so about a week later, Espen went to Oslo for an audition and screen test. He got the part, to the amazement of no one who had ever seen him act."

"What role was this?" Bethany asked.

"It was a part in *Forever and a Dream*. Remember that old teen soap opera? Espen played the mysterious newcomer to the high school who had a dark past. We were glued to our screens every week, watching him. It was all so exciting." Anita's eyes hardened. "And then he gave an interview to one of the local celebrity magazines. Now, I get that journalists don't often get all the details right and sometimes leave stuff out or twist words in order to make a story more interesting. But Espen told this magazine how glad he was to be working with real professionals in Oslo, and how jealous and uncultured provincials were holding him back."

Bethany winced. Had Espen really spoken like that about his old friends?

Anita crossed her arms. "He would never have been noticed if these so-called jealous provincials hadn't put together a theater group that he happened to stumble into. We couldn't believe what we were reading, and everyone was in shock when we talked about the article at our rehearsal one evening. Lukas said they must have taken Espen's words out of context. If it had just been the one article, I think many of the group might have eventually come around.

"Then he appeared on that magazine show on TV and said the same thing. They invited him on, gushing about this exciting young talent from Finnmark, and how there was talk of the scriptwriters expanding on his part because he'd become so popular. He talks about how hard he's worked in order to get noticed, and that people don't realize how much dedication and focus it gets to land a role. He gave no credit to his brother or to the drama team, or even to his casting agent for opening the door for him. It was all about how hard he'd worked. By then, all of us were done with him."

Bethany shook her head. Could she believe all this?

"The only one in the group who didn't appear to be miffed was Lukas," Anita said. "That's always puzzled me.

The agent only came on his account to see him playing Shylock. And he was amazing that night. He had the audience in tears when he gave his famous 'has not a Jew eyes' speech. I asked him point blank whether he wasn't upset that Espen had stolen his chance. Lukas said it wasn't his time. And it seems it never was Lukas's time, because he eventually left to go the university, and as far as I know he never seriously pursued acting again. As for Espen, I guess you could say the rest is history. After a brief run with *Forever and a Dream*, he did that movie that was screened in Cannes and then landed his first Hollywood role. He never looked back, and he left the rest of us in the dust."

Bethany wasn't sure what to reply, so she settled on, "Wow."

Anita smiled. "You know, now that I tell you all this, it all sounds so far away and petty. It was an enormous deal for us and we were so indignant. But in the grand scheme of things, what did it matter? Apart from Espen and Lukas, none of us ever had a serious shot at making it as actors. Most of us went on to have great lives. We may not have set the world on fire, but we were okay. But this isn't a town that forgives easily. Espen's words really stung since his family wasn't originally from here, but moved from Trondheim or wherever it was. He made it sound like he was buried in this backwater where the jealous inbreeds tried to hold him back. Oh, and he ghosted me, as well."

"Did he? That wasn't cool."

"No, it wasn't. Especially since I was head over heels for him and he was my first—well, never mind about that. I never heard from him again after he went to Oslo. But it is what it is. I was much better off with my husband." Anita held up her hand. "No offense, of course."

"None taken," Bethany said. "I'm glad to hear you've been happy."

"Thanks. So, that's my tale about Espen Meland. And if you're interested, I have some pictures of him."

"I'd love to see them," Bethany said.

"I dug them up after Lukas called me. The theater group's photographer took snapshots of the cast of the *Merchant of Venice*. I'll be back in a minute."

Bethany sat back in her chair. There was so much to process from what Anita had said. Espen hadn't behaved well, but it sounded like he'd just been a bit of a jerk, like ninety percent of all teenagers occasionally were. She could weave this into her manuscript and give her editor the nuance she wanted. Something else nagged at her, though, which she couldn't quite put a finger on.

Anita returned holding a thick envelope. "Here you go. The Oscar-winning Espen Meland in his one and only appearance with the Havdal Theater Troupe."

Bethany cycled through the photos. A fresh-faced Anita stood next to Espen. He wore a dandified costume that might have come across as ridiculous on a less confident person. Even through the picture, he carried off the Elizabethan attire well, posing at just the right angle to make it look elegant.

Lukas, in black, scowled at the camera, in a stooped posture that made him look like an elderly man, although he couldn't have been much older than twenty.

"See what I mean?" Anita pointed at the picture. "Lukas was Shylock. That photo still gives me the chills. If you didn't know him, it was hard to believe he was a nineteen-year-old kid."

"Yes, I see." Bethany stared a moment longer before turning to the next picture. Espen again, this time on the stage. Her editor would love these. She looked up at Anita. "Would it be too much to ask–"

"You want to borrow them for your book? I'm open to that. But just so everything is above board, I'd prefer the request to come from your publisher. They can send me an email and I'll look over the terms."

"Of course," Bethany said.

They chatted for a while longer until Anita said, "I've got to pick up my daughter from school. Did you and Espen have children?"

Bethany shook her head. "No." The question didn't sting as much as it

used to, but it was still a tender spot. Being the mother of Espen's child was one of the dreams she'd had to bury along with her husband.

She got to her feet. "Thanks so much for making the time to speak with me."

"You're welcome. I was hesitant at first, but I'm glad I did. You know, talking through it helped me realize how long ago it was, how far I've come, and how glad I am that my life turned out the way it did. So, thank you. And best of luck with your book."

Back in her car, Bethany ran through what Espen had told her about his early break. He'd never mentioned the drama group, or how

Lukas had been involved in acting as well.

Then the thing that had been niggling at the back of her mind hit her. Espen had told her he'd landed his first role when *Forever and a Dream* had an open casting and he'd auditioned on a whim with no help from an agent. That didn't line up with what Anita had said.

An uneasiness squirmed in the pit of her stomach. Had Espen lied? Or perhaps he'd misremembered what happened, being such a long time ago. For that matter, Anita may not have gotten the details right, either.

There was one way she could find out for sure. Lukas would know.

Chapter Nine

UKAS KNEW THIS WASN'T a good idea in his condition, and he would much rather be in bed. But he'd promised Bethany he would search his attic for family mementos she could use in her book, and he intended to keep his word.

Had she already met with Anita Ilseth? He wondered how that conversation had gone. Anita wouldn't have sugarcoated her opinion of Espen.

He dragged himself upstairs to the middle guest bedroom of his home.

The attic could be accessed via a trap-door in the ceiling. A retractable ladder leading to the attic was attached to the inside of the door.

He found the pole that he needed to open the door, but his coordination was so sketchy that it took a couple of tries to hook the trap door's ring-shaped handle.

Was there any part of his body this blasted Lyme didn't affect? He was more than a week into his course of antibiotics and he didn't feel any better. Half his face was still frozen and his energy was at its lowest ebb. He used to pride himself on his ability to function on only five hours of sleep a night. But these days, he was ready to collapse into bed by seven in the

evening, and it was a struggle to get up before eight.

There was no way he'd be able to do much more than a quick glance in the attic tonight. He was already running on his last reserves of energy.

He pulled the trapdoor open and grabbed the ladder as it slid down. His arm muscles trembled and the headache that had plagued him for days throbbed behind his ears.

He really shouldn't be going into the attic alone, with no one else in the house. What would happen if he lost his balance and fell off the ladder? He might be lying here all night before anyone noticed he was missing. No, wait. It was Friday and his PA wasn't coming in until Monday. He could be here all weekend. This was how empty his life had become. He could end up as one of those lonely old men who die alone, missed by no one, bodies rotting in their homes until someone reported the foul smell to the authorities.

He clutched a rung at shoulder height, holding it so tight his knuckles turned white. If he was careful, he would be fine. He stepped slowly up the ladder.

He made it into the attic, groping in the dark for the pull switch to turn on the light. The hot, stuffy air hung heavy with dust particles that swirled in the light of a bare, swinging lightbulb.

Moving away from the trapdoor, he rose slowly. He could stand upright in the center of the attic, but as he walked forward, the ceiling sloped downward and he would need to crouch.

It must have been at least ten years since he was last here. Boxes filled every corner, but there was a clear path down the middle of the attic. The bulb didn't light up the entire space, so he pulled down a torch that hung near the trapdoor.

Where should he start looking? His mother's things probably lay wherever they'd been put when he and Kai had cleared out her house. Those were the boxes where he'd most likely find family albums and mementos from Espen's childhood. Perhaps it would be best to start at the back and work his way toward the middle of the room. He stepped forward, then stopped.

Espen had also asked him to hold some boxes when he and Bethany had moved to the US. Might those contain anything useful? Lukas swung the torch around. A couple of meters ahead sat a group of cardboard boxes. Those could be the items he was looking for.

He aimed a beam of light into the box and peered inside. A tennis racket, a few tennis balls in cylindrical boxes, some free weights. Nothing else in there but random exercise equipment. He turned to a box next to that one. Several files and documents were stacked inside. That didn't look like it would contain the information Bethany was looking for. She wanted mementos from way back.

An envelope caught his eye. It was marked with an official-looking seal. He looked closer. It was a letter addressed to Espen from Drammen Hospital. Lukas pulled the envelope out of the box. He set the torch down and extracted the letter.

Dear Mr. Meland,

We are pleased to confirm your appointment for a sterilization procedure on May 5th, 2002.

The words blurred as he tried to read on. Head throbbing, Lukas refolded the letter and stuffed it back into the envelope.

Espen had had a vasectomy. And by the date on the letter, he'd done it after he and Bethany were already married. But that wasn't possible. Anyone who knew Bethany also knew how much she wanted a family. She talked about it all the time.

Could Espen have had this done without telling her? Surely not. That was a level of cruelty beyond anything his brother was capable of. And yet...

An image flashed through Lukas's mind of Bethany playing with her little niece on Eline's first Christmas, saying, "I can't wait till we have one of our own. Children make Christmas so much more special." Espen had looked on and smiled.

Lukas pulled out the letter and stared at the date, replaying the Christmas memory in his mind. Bethany made that comment before Espen had had this procedure. But why would he have had a vasectomy after his wife had let everyone know how much she was looking forward to being a mother?

He slipped the letter into his pocket. There was no reason to assume the worst. Espen might have reversed the vasectomy. That was possible, right? There was no way he could be so callous and deceptive. And Lukas should not be speculating on the fertility of another man and his wife.

The air in the attic was stuffy and close, and his head felt like someone was trying to drill their way out of his forehead.

He'd hoped to get more done here, but he'd slammed into a wall. He'd better get out before his fatigue caused muscle tremors and made it dangerous to climb down the ladder.

Lukas hung the torch back in its place and headed for the trapdoor.

His quick search had sapped the little energy he had, and he'd barely made a dent in checking out what was in these boxes. Going through everything would take him days, or even weeks, unless someone else could come here and help him look.

As his feet hit the floor, his phone rang.

He pulled it out of his pocket, smiling as he glanced at the screen. "Hey, Kai. How are you?"

"We're all good. But it sounds like you're not. Bethany told Lisa you have Lyme disease and your face is paralyzed or something?"

Lukas sighed. News traveled way too fast. "Yes, that's right."

"Why didn't you tell us?"

Lukas raised the ladder and stuck the door pole in the room's corner. "I didn't want you to worry. Besides, you're thousands of miles away. What would you have done?"

"We could have at least prayed for you. Maybe arranged with people from church to bring meals around. You don't have to be Mr. Tough Guy

Lone Ranger. You can let other people help once in a while."

Irritation sparked within Lukas. "I'm doing fine, okay?"

Kai, with his gambling addiction, should be the last person to give Lukas lectures on how to behave. After several years with Gambler's Anonymous, Kai had gotten back on track, including a fresh lease of life in his marriage. But Lukas wasn't used to going to his younger brother for help. Especially when for years Kai had been the flaky basket case of the family while Lukas had held everything together.

He forced his tone to remain even. "The doctor caught it in time and has things under control. I'm on a course of antibiotics." Although the meds weren't acting as fast as he'd hoped. "There isn't any need to worry anyone."

"Okay, okay, if you say so. We're just concerned, okay? A friend of mine had Lyme, and it hit him pretty hard."

Great. And now Lukas was feeling guilty for snapping at his brother, who'd only wanted to show concern. "Thanks."

"Have you taken some time off work?" Kai asked.

"Yes, I have. My friend Gunnar has taken over some of my most urgent engagements, which is giving me some breathing space."

"That's great to hear. And how's it going digging up that stuff Bethany needs? Did you manage to find something useful for her?"

"I lined up one interview, so hopefully she's got something out of that. And I was just up in the attic looking for photo albums and stuff like that, but it's pretty slow going." Lukas made a face. "I just piled things in there with no thought of what a headache it would be to sort everything out."

"Maybe you should get someone to help," Kai said. "Bethany could do it. She has an idea of the kind of stuff she needs."

Lukas frowned. Have Bethany up here to help? "That's a thought," he said. "I'll keep that in mind."

Kai sighed. "I'd better get back to work. I called between lectures. Lisa sends her love. God bless."

"Thanks," Lukas said. He ended the call.

Kai had suggested asking Bethany to help out with the search through the attic. A second pair of hands would make a massive difference in the time it took to search through the storage crates.

He'd better call her now before he lost his nerve.

He dialed her number, speaking quickly when she answered. "Hey, Bethany. I was in my attic today, but I soon realized I can't sort through all that stuff on my own, unless you're willing to wait weeks for what you need. Do you have time to take a look for yourself?"

Her voice was pitched high with surprise. "Sure. Of course I can look. When were you thinking?"

"Any day that isn't Sunday. And as long as it's between ten in the morning and four in the afternoon."

"How about tomorrow at eleven?"

He nodded. "That'll be fine. See you then."

As he slipped the phone back into his pocket, his fingers brushed against the envelope he'd slipped in there. He froze. He'd just asked Bethany to look through the attic. What if she'd stumbled across this letter? If she didn't know about Espen's vasectomy, he would not be responsible for causing her that kind of pain. Not if he could help it.

He went into his office, stumbling as he got to his desk. His fatigue was bone deep. Pulling Espen's letter out of his pocket, he slid it into a document folder on his desk. He'd dispose of it tomorrow. Right now, he needed to lie down.

Chapter Ten

ETHANY PARKED HER CAR in Lukas's driveway on Saturday morning. She stepped out, pausing to drink in a deep breath of air.

Spring had finally come to Berghaven, drenching Lukas's home in bright sunshine. He lived at the end of a cul-de-sac on a finger of land that jutted out into the sea, allowing ocean views at both dawn and sunset. If she had her pick of properties in town, Bethany would have chosen this one.

Lukas met her at the door, his gray cable-knit sweater hanging off his tall, gaunt frame. There were dark smudges under his eyes and when he smiled, it was still with only half his face. The Bell's Palsy was still persisting, then. He looked like he could use a good meal and a nap.

But his handshake was warm and firm. "Hi. Come on in."

He led the way down the hallway, facing her when they got to his living room. "I tried to poke around in the attic yesterday and quickly realized what a huge job it would be. Shall we jump straight in? I'm assuming you don't want to lose any time."

"Okay," she said, pushing aside the questions she'd been itching to ask him following her conversation with Anita.

They walked into an upstairs bedroom. Huge glass windows made the most of the sea view.

"Excuse me." Reaching behind her, he grabbed a pole that stood behind the door. "This is one of those attics you get into via a ladder. I'll get it down if you'll step toward the window."

He pulled the ladder down. Placing a foot on the first rung, he looked down at her. "I'll go in first, but you might want to come up, too, and see just how much stuff there is, so you'll know what we're up against."

Waiting until he reached the attic, Bethany climbed the ladder after him.

She straightened up in the stuffy air, whistling at the expanse of crates and boxes. "I see what you mean about this taking weeks if you did it on your own. There's so much stuff in here."

"A lot of it is what we brought from Mama's house and just shoved it all up here."

Bethany looked at his face. Spending hours up here crouched over boxes wouldn't do his health any good. "Can we take these out and look at them a few at a time?"

"I was thinking the same thing. If you'll go back down, I'll hand you one of the smaller crates. Anything that's too bulky or unwieldy, we can look at up here. I don't want any mishaps involving ladders and heavy boxes."

She climbed back down into the bedroom. Her feet planted on the floor, Bethany reached up and grabbed the first plastic crate as Lukas lowered it from the attic. She shoved it next to the bed and went back to receive the second one. In a couple of minutes, about ten crates stood in the room.

Lukas climbed down the ladder. Face pale, he leaned against the wall. "These are enough to start with. We can take on another batch when we've seen what we have." His hand shook as he placed it on his hip.

She stepped toward him. "Are you okay?" He should be resting, not hauling boxes from the attic.

"I'm fine." His firm tone and the tightness around his jaw didn't invite any further questions. He turned to the crate closest to him.

She lifted the lid on a crate in front of her, smiling as her hand brushed over the glossy cover of a twenty-five-year-old edition of *Norsk Ukeblad*. Her mother-in-law Berit had subscribed to the weekly women's magazine for decades. The crate was full of them. At any other time Bethany would have loved to page through the magazines and see how prices, fashions, and agony aunt's advice had changed through the years.

Today, though, she was here with one purpose—to find information that could add more meat to her biography of her husband.

She put the lid back on the crate. "This one has copies of *Norsk Ukeblad*. What do you have there?"

Lukas shoved his crate aside. "Seems to be nothing but old Christmas decorations."

He pulled another one toward him and popped the lid off. "This looks more promising. It's got some albums."

"Really? Let me see." Bethany crossed over to where Lukas sat. Kneeling, she bent over the open crate and lifted out a thick black book. Her pulse rate ticked up. "It's a scrapbook of press clippings."

Someone, most likely Berit, had cut out magazine and newspaper articles and pasted them onto the album.

Lukas leaned closer, his spicy cologne wafting to Bethany's nostrils. "That's a writeup about his first TV role. I had no idea Mama kept this."

Bethany turned the page, revealing a spread with several articles and a movie ticket stub.

Lukas chuckled. "These are all about *Elemental Fire*, Espen's first big screen role. He would have been, what, seventeen? Looks like Mama saved her ticket. I think the movie was only shown in Scandinavian theaters."

"There's a letter here." Bethany pointed at the page. She read the hand-written note aloud. "'Congratulations. Great things lie in store for you. Morten.' Who's that?"

Lukas peered at the note. "Morten Petersen. He was Espen's first agent. The one who discovered him and helped him get his first role."

Bethany's heart lurched. Was this the same agent Anita talked about? That would confirm her story. So, Espen had lied about how he got his first role. Why would he do that?

"There's a picture of the two of them," Lukas said.

Bethany examined the candid snapshot of a handsome gangly youth, blond hair flopping over his forehead, his arm around the shoulder of a shorter, middle-aged man. Her eyes moistened. This was Espen at the start of his career, the world lying at his feet. He would have had no idea how big that career would get, or that he wouldn't live to see his forties.

"I think I have his contact details." Lukas sat upright.

"What?"

"I might still have Morten's contact details. We kept in touch over the years. Christmas cards and so on. I don't know why I didn't think of him when you first asked about people who knew Espen at the start of his career."

Bethany scanned Lukas's face for any signs of jealousy or awkwardness, but didn't see any. "Maybe you could clear this up for me. When I talked to Anita, she said Espen had an agent who discovered him and helped him line up his first proper role."

"Yes. That was Morten."

"But Espen told me he landed his first role via an open casting call without an agent. I looked up an old *Vanity Fair* interview, and he said the same thing. I don't understand how both his version and what you and Anita say can be true."

Lukas didn't answer straight away. He pulled another scrapbook out of the crate and leafed through a couple of pages. Sighing, he raised his gaze back to Bethany. "It's not my story to tell. I'll get in touch with Morten and see if he wants to speak with you. He can tell you himself."

"Thanks." Bethany laid the scrapbook aside. "Could I ask about something that is your story to tell?"

His posture stiffened. "All right. What do you want to know?"

Bethany drew in a deep breath. Best to lay it all out. "Anita said you were the leading light of the theater group before Espen came along."

"The leading light?" His mouth curved in the half-smile his facial paralysis allowed.

"She said you were very talented and everyone thought the casting agent was coming all the way to Havdal to see you. But Espen was the one he invited to audition. Is that accurate?"

Lukas rubbed his forehead. "I had some ability. And, yes, when we put on a production of the *Merchant of Venice*, we knew a casting agent was coming."

"Did you want a career in acting?"

He shrugged. "Yes. I also wanted to win a medal at the Winter Olympics and go on a date with Tyra Banks. My point is, I was nineteen. Most of my ambitions weren't realistic, and I knew they weren't. I was glad Espen got that opportunity. I was a competent actor, but he had something special. Some of the other people in the theater group got offended on my behalf and started saying Espen stole my shot at fame and fortune. Did Anita say something along those lines?"

Bethany nodded.

"I imagined she would," Lukas said. "And Espen didn't help matters when he went on TV and said some unflattering things about our town. But I didn't hold any of that against him. It wasn't my spot. We both had a chance to impress the agent on that day, and Espen's talent couldn't be denied."

Bethany stared at Lukas. Was he being honest? Could he really be so devoid of ego that he didn't mind his upstart little brother eclipsing him in a field that had previously been his?

He looked back at her, his gray-eyed gaze steady. "Espen deserved to get noticed that day. And he proved repeatedly that he had a real gift. As far

as that audition goes, I don't hold anything against him."

He stood and put a scrapbook back
into the box. "I could use a cup of coffee. Do you want one, too?"

"Yes, thanks." Bethany watched
Lukas leave the room. He sounded
sincere. But as a person who made her
living with words, she could tell when
someone was choosing theirs carefully. *As far as that audition goes.* Did
that mean there might be other things
Lukas held against his brother?

She flipped through the rest of the
scrapbook, past page after page of
press clippings and snapshots of
Espen.

Lukas appeared in the doorway.
"I've put the coffee on. And I got in

touch with Espen's former agent, Morten Petersen. He's in Havdal."

Bethany's back straightened. "Will he talk to me?"

"He will. But he's terminally ill in a hospice." Lukas combed a hand through his hair, a crease deepening between his eyebrows. "He didn't say it in so many words, but if you want to interview him, you'd better make it soon. Can you talk to him early next week?"

Bethany got to her feet. "Monday. I can make time on Monday."

"Good. I'll let him know. And I hope it's not a problem, but he asked whether I can come along, too."

"That's not a problem for me at all. Would you be okay with that?"

He nodded. "Yes. I'm not sure what he might have to say to me, but I'd love to see him one last time. I'll call him back right away."

Chapter Eleven

ETHANY HAD NEVER BEEN to a place where people came to die. The waiting room of St. Olaf's Hospice smelled of disinfectant and faded flowers. The hospice itself was a waiting room of sorts. People were marking time until they left this earth.

A rail thin woman sat at a window, staring out at the garden where daffodils bloomed.

Bethany shuddered as Lukas introduced himself to the receptionist. A chill lay over the room, at odds with the bright spring weather outside. A young family gathered around an elderly man on the patio. Bundled up in a coat and scarves, his gray skin contrasted with the rosy cheeks of the toddler who sat in his lap. A middle-aged woman sobbed into a tissue while a man took pictures of the patient and the child.

The receptionist said, "Mr. Petersen is expecting you. This way, please."

She led Bethany and Lukas to a room at the end of a hallway. Knocking lightly, she poked her head around the door. "Mr. Petersen, you have some visitors."

Bethany followed Lukas into the room, which resembled a hotel room apart from the hospital bed in the center and the frail man who lay propped up in it. Only by pushing her imagination hard could she see any trace of the robust-looking man who'd been in the picture with Espen.

Morten Petersen's cracked lips stretched in a smile as he raised a bony hand in greeting. "It's good to see you, Lukas. Thank you for coming."

The man's pale blue gaze turned to Bethany. "You're Espen's widow. Beatrice, was it?"

"Bethany."

"Oh, yes, Bethany. Excuse me. Please have a seat. I understand you're writing a book about Espen?"

Bethany sat on one of the two chairs next to the bed. "Yes, I'm writing his biography. Right now I'm trying to fill in some gaps around the time he was just beginning to find success. So, I really appreciate your agreeing to speak with me."

Mr. Petersen's gaze flickered at Lukas. "If you'd approached me a year ago, I would probably have declined to be involved in your project. But terminal illness has a way of changing one's perspective."

Bethany stared at him, unsure how to answer. "Oh. I'm sorry."

"No need to be sorry. The end comes to us all, sooner or later. And since I have advance warning of mine, it's given me time to prepare and reflect, which is something not everyone gets." He coughed heavily, doubling up, bright spots of red blooming on his cheeks.

Bethany jumped to her feet. "Can I get you anything? A drink of water? A nurse?"

Shaking his head, Mr. Petersen dragged in a ragged breath. "No. Thank you. It'll pass. It's passing already." He coughed a couple more times. "There. I'm fine now. As I was saying, a couple of years ago, I probably wouldn't have agreed to speak with you. I had a major bone to pick with Espen."

Bethany sat, pulling her notebook and pen from her bag. "Do you mind if I record our conversation?"

"Not at all. I believe in solid documentation. What would you like to know?"

Bethany clicked her recorder on. "Could we start with how you came to know Espen?"

Mr. Petersen leaned back into his pillows. "I was based in Oslo, but I grew up in Havdal. I liked to look for undiscovered talent up here in the northern districts as a way of giving back to my own community. I'd heard of a promising young actor who'd started up a theater group in my own hometown, so I was very curious to check out what they were doing. When I watched the group perform the *Merchant of Venice*, Espen blew me away."

He looked at Lukas. "You were wonderful, too, of course, but the particular role I had in mind called for a younger actor."

Lukas inclined his head.

"I signed Espen on straight away and invited him to Oslo to audition for *Forever and a Dream*. His part wasn't a big one, but it got him noticed. I helped him land more roles on a couple of other Norway-based movies and TV shows. He did *Elemental Fire*, which was his first big screen role."

Bethany scribbled in her notebook. It was confirmed, then. Espen had lied to her and to *Vanity Fair* about his early career. But why had he done that? Thankfully, Mr. Petersen was happy to talk without further prompting.

"Very early on, though, I could see Espen had Hollywood potential, given his talent and his work ethic. People can say whatever they like about Espen Meland, but the boy wasn't afraid to work hard at his craft, and he was a perfectionist.

"So, I advised him to hire an English tutor. He could speak the language, of course, but I wanted him to be flawless. He had an ear for language and he worked like a machine. He did so well that within six months he was also studying with a dialect coach to perfect his English and American accents so he could swap between them at will."

Mr. Petersen paused, shaking his head. "I've never worked with anyone so gifted in that way. It's what has held so many of our actors back from making it in Hollywood. They can't lose their accents and sound like a native speaker of English. But Espen could."

Bethany smiled. Espen's mastery of English dialects was one of the things journalists and film critics found so astounding. There was a YouTube video of him still online, in which he ran through a monologue, cycling through over fifteen regional English, Australian, and American accents.

Mr. Petersen took a sip of water and cleared his throat. "For about a year, Espen did nothing but study English and work. *Forever and a Dream* extended his contract because he was such a fan favorite, and he also shot *Elemental Fire II*. And then I thought he might be ready to try for his first English-speaking role. To be certain, I invited him for dinner with some British friends of mine who were visiting. I didn't tell them he was an actor, but just asked him to speak English with them. We spent the evening eating and chatting. None of them realized he wasn't a native speaker. That's when I knew he was ready to try for his first Hollywood role."

Bethany glanced at Lukas. He was looking downward at his hands, which were clasped across his knees.

She faced Mr. Petersen again. "So, at this point in his career, what was Espen like as a client?"

"He was like a sponge, absorbing everything around him, soaking up knowledge. We would talk for hours about movies and books, and I felt he valued my advice. I saw him as a son. And I thought he shared a similar closeness to me, but I was wrong. Wait, I shouldn't get ahead of myself."

Bethany's heart sank. Now came the Espen bashing part.

Mr. Petersen said, "When I was sure he had the English thing nailed, I pulled every string I had to get a friend to allow Espen to audition for a role in the US. It wasn't big, but it was Hollywood, and the movie had some respected industry names behind it. I traveled there with him and he did the audition. He didn't get the part, although he did really well. They decided they needed an older actor. We weren't discouraged, though, because Espen got such great feedback.

"I had to come back to Norway, but Espen remained in Hollywood, staying with some friends of mine who had a son about his age. The plan was he'd audition for a few more roles and see if anything came up. For a while, it seemed nothing was happening. So, I lined up a couple of roles for him here just to keep him earning and building his resume. Then I heard through the grapevine that he was up for a really

big part. The kind every actor dreams about."

"Was that *The Color of Love*?" Bethany asked.

"It was, indeed. The audition was grueling, and he had to go through several rounds of callbacks, but he got the part. And that's when things began to go downhill between me and him."

Bethany's gut twisted. "What do you mean?"

"As his agent, I was supposed to get a twelve percent cut of whatever he was paid. It's standard in the movie business. I'd introduced Espen to Cameron Fontaine, the casting director of *The Color of Love*. The movie was a huge hit, as you know. It launched Espen's career and put him firmly on the radar in Hollywood. But he never paid me a penny. I asked him about it, and he gave me some wishy washy excuse about how he'd not needed my representation to get the part. Completely ignoring how it was through my contacts and my influence that he got a foot through the door.

"Anyway, a couple of weeks after I called him out on it, I got a letter from him, saying once our contract was over, he had no intention of renewing our professional relationship. He mentioned nothing about the money I was due for helping him land *The Color of Love*. I could handle being dropped—it hurt since I thought we were close, but it happens all the time

in this business. But I wanted to be paid what I was owed. I contacted him a couple of months later. Nothing. He completely ghosted me and then changed his number, I assume, because my calls always went straight to voicemail after that. *The Color of Love* exploded, and Espen was in both sequels.

"My lawyer said I had grounds to sue, and I seriously considered it. But then I thought, a fifty-year-old man trying to sue a teenager just starting out? Not a good look. Time went on and as Espen's star continued to rise, things changed. He wasn't a fresh-faced teen anymore. He was now an A-list star, and the optics wouldn't be so bad if I went after him for what he owed me. I very nearly did. And then the cancer hit the first time. Suddenly, settling old scores seemed a lot less important. While I was going through treatment, Espen died in that accident, underlining for me how fleeting life is. I got better, and my lawyer said I could make a claim on Espen's estate."

He chuckled. "And I thought, now you want me to go after a widow and kids? I fired my lawyer."

Bethany managed a smile. "There are no kids."

"Well, you get my drift." He shrugged. "Anyway, just when I might have been tempted to sue again, the cancer made a comeback and here we are. Even if I sued and by some mira-

cle lived long enough to see a win, what's the point? My children are well into their fifties and settled. I'm not going to fight just to enrich the lawyers."

"I'm so sorry things turned out that way."

Mr. Petersen shrugged. "I've had ungrateful clients before. It goes with the territory. But it cut a different way with Espen. He felt like family, and I put a lot into him. So, yeah, I took it personally when he dropped me like a rock the second I was no longer useful to him. I was dispensable."

Dispensable. A chill passed over Bethany's heart as she remembered the nights when Espen was out late "networking" but the morning tabloids published pictures of him exiting a super-hip club or bar, a barely clothed starlet draped around him. As Bethany put on weight and no longer qualified as arm candy, Espen asked her less and less often to attend events with him. She was probably dispensable, too.

Mr. Petersen peered at Bethany. "So, that's my story. I'm sorry if that's not what you wanted to hear about your late husband."

She forced her lips into the shape of a smile. "I'm getting used to hearing that kind of thing."

He laughed. "To hear Espen tell it in his media interviews, he sprang fully formed onto the Hollywood scene. No previous stepping stones, no helping hand along the way, no mentor steering him toward language lessons and picking the right scripts to look at. No mention of the hours we spent talking about what mattered to him and how he wanted to grow in his craft. I took what he said, the potential I saw in him, and drew up a career map. And even though he dropped me, it sounds like he followed my plan to a tee. I advised him to build on blockbuster success by branching out into more challenging indie roles in order to avoid typecasting.

"Don't get me wrong–I'm not upset that he dropped me. He was fully within his rights to move on to a different agent, or no agent at all. What I didn't like was the way he did it, the disrespect he showed, the complete lack of acknowledgment about how I helped him on his way. Not to mention the money he stiffed me out of. Given the franchise that came out of *The Color of Love*, Espen owed me a six-figure fee. But I'm not bitter." Mr. Petersen laughed, a barking chuckle that ended in a long coughing fit.

Wiping his mouth with a tissue, he settled back onto his pillows. "So, there you have it. My association with Espen Meland didn't end so well. But you don't have to take my word for it. Lukas here knows. I met him several times while Espen and I were still working together. Lukas didn't approve of what his brother did, and he and I stayed in touch over the years."

He glanced at Lukas, who met his gaze and nodded.

Mr. Petersen went on. "I also have documentation about the work I did with Espen, the career plan I made for him, communication with his language tutors, correspondence with my lawyer about the compensation suit I ended up not filing. Plus, of course, Espen's own documented media interviews where he makes no mention of how I helped him get his start. I'm something of a pack rat and kept a hold of all these records. My daughter can get them to you if you like. I don't know how you plan to use it all, but I'm happy to turn it all over."

"Thank you," Bethany said. "I appreciate it. I'm not sure how it'll fit into my book, either, and it'll be subject to my editors, but I'll do all I can to give you credit for how you helped Espen."

Mr. Petersen's smile lit up his face. "That's all I want. You're a decent human being. It's clear Espen didn't find you in Hollywood. Where did he meet you?"

"My best friend married his brother. There was supposed to be a big wedding, and he came over for that, before it got canceled and they eloped instead." Bethany shut her mouth to stop the babbling. Mr. Petersen didn't need to hear the details about her friends' wedding plans.

"That explains it. You're a regular girl next door. You definitely don't fit the movie star wife mold." He pulled his water toward him with a shaky hand and drew a sip through the straw. "I don't mean to be rude, but I'm exhausted and my pain meds are starting to wear off."

Bethany clicked off her recorder and slid it into her bag. "Yes, of course. Thanks for giving us this time. You've been very helpful."

"You're welcome. I'll ask my daughter to send you all that correspondence I told you about. If you're going to put it into your book, you'll want documentation. I left it in a folder at home. Feel free to call if you want any additional details."

Bethany shook Mr. Petersen's dry, bony hand, her throat aching as she realized she'd probably never see him again. Why had Espen treated him so shabbily? There was a whole side to her husband she didn't know. And it was making her increasingly uneasy.

Chapter Twelve

UKAS STRUGGLED TO KEEP up with Bethany as she strode out of the hospice. His energy was still low and the woman could move, despite her flimsy-looking shoes.

By the time he got to the parking lot, she was next to her car, jabbing her key fob. She'd driven them both here, sparing him the drain on his energy.

Bethany yanked the rear passenger door open. She shoved her purse and tote bag inside, slammed the door, and flopped onto the driver's seat.

As Lukas slid into the front passenger seat, Bethany gripped the steering wheel, staring straight ahead. Her lips were pressed tightly together.

Glancing at her face, he snapped his seat belt into place. "Hey, are you okay?"

She squeezed her eyes shut and blew out a puff of air through rounded lips. "I should have asked Mr. Petersen whether he wanted us to pray for him. I don't know whether he's a person of faith, but I wish I'd brought it up."

He stared at her. It can't have been easy to hear what Mr. Petersen had told her about Espen. But she'd been polite and professional. And now she was worried about praying for him?

Her concern pricked his conscience. "We could pray for him now."

"Okay." She reached for his hand.

His large hand dwarfed hers, and for a moment he was distracted by the softness of her skin and how cool her fingers felt. Clearing his throat, he prayed for Mr. Petersen's comfort, asking God to open the elderly man's heart to his grace as he prepared for eternity.

Opening her eyes, Bethany started the engine and shifted into reverse. But instead of backing out of her parking spot, she turned the ignition off.

"Something else is clearly bothering you," Lukas said.

"You mean besides learning how Espen was a complete jerk to the mentor who launched his entire career?"

He rubbed his chin. "That must have been hard to listen to."

"I'm sorry. I just need a moment." She tilted her face downward, pressing the heels of her palms into her eyes.

It hurt to see her like this. And there was nothing he could do to help. He twisted his fingers in his lap, casting about for something, anything to say to make it better.

She straightened in her seat, blinking rapidly. "Sorry."

"Why are you apologizing? Today's been hard."

"Could you check if there's a tissue in the glove compartment?"

He pulled it open and rummaged around, his fingers colliding with a small travel pack of Kleenex.

"Thanks." She took it from him and wiped her eyes. "This might sound silly, but it feels like I'm losing Espen all over again. It's as though there were good sides of him that I have to bury and mourn because I've suddenly learned they're dead. Even if they never really existed." She held up her hands and shook her head. "That made sense in my head, but now it sounds really crazy."

"That's not crazy at all." His heart ached for her. All she'd done wrong was love his fool of a brother. "You've carried an image of Espen in your heart, so it's normal to be sad to lose part of what you loved about him."

Her deep brown eyes softened. "You totally get it. That's exactly how I feel." She touched his arm, making his heart swell.

But if she was this rattled after hearing just a fraction of Espen's misdeeds, how would she take it if she knew more? What if she found out about things he'd done that affected her directly? Like his vasectomy? That knowledge would crush her, and he didn't want to be there if it happened. He certainly didn't want to be the one to drop the anvil on her head.

A phone chimed, and Bethany twisted in her seat. "Oh, that's mine."

She reached behind her for her purse and pulled out her phone.

"Hi, Tina. What?" Her jaw dropped. "Please tell me you're joking."

Lukas watched her as she listened to whoever was on the other side of the line.

She shook her head. "I told you it was urgent. Why did you wait so long? What are we supposed to do? You know what? I've got a long drive ahead and I can't deal with this right now. I'll talk to you later."

She shoved the phone back into her purse and slammed a fist on the side of her seat.

"What's the matter?" Lukas asked. He'd never seen her this agitated.

"It's my sister-in-law. We're planning a surprise party for my mother's seventy-fifth birthday. Tina was supposed to book a venue for the party, but instead of confirming with them last week like we agreed, she's left it until now. So, of course, they're not available. And now I've got to find a place that can host fifty guests at just two weeks' notice."

"What kind of party? A sit-down meal?"

She shook her head. "No, I was thinking of a cocktail party so my mother can circulate around the guests."

"If you're stuck, you could have it at my place." The invitation popped out before he thought it through.

Her eyes rounded. "Are you serious?"

"Sure. I've got a large yard. Especially since you said it'll be a cocktail party and not a sit-down buffet."

"Wow, I don't know what to say. You're such a lifesaver. Are you sure it's okay? I'll organize caterers and people to help decorate and clean up afterward so it'll be as little bother to you as possible."

Being able to help her made him feel ten feet tall. "Yes, it's okay. What date is it?"

"The sixteenth. Lukas, I can't thank you enough. I'll talk to the person doing the decorations and the caterers."

She started the engine. "We'd better get back to Berghaven so I can get this interview transcribed."

And he needed to check his calendar and rearrange any prior plans he had for the sixteenth. He would make sure Bethany didn't have any further worries about the venue for her mother's party.

Chapter Thirteen

THE NEXT SATURDAY MORNING, Bethany was back at Lukas's place to go through the boxes from the attic again.

They'd developed a system that worked reasonably well. He would lower some crates from the attic, and they'd look through the contents. This morning they'd been through ten crates already, filled with more of Berit's women's magazine collection and sewing and crafting supplies.

Bethany settled in front of the latest box, her pulse ticking up as she opened it. These looked like albums. She turned to the first page. It was a picture of three children posing for a formal professional portrait. Two small boys aged about five and three smiled for the camera in starchy-looking sailor suits. A baby sat on the older boy's lap.

Bethany's gaze traced over the eldest boy's face. He was an adorable child with large gray eyes. She looked up at Lukas, who sat a few meters away, looking through another crate. "Where was this picture taken?"

He glanced up with the same gray eyes as the boy in the picture. "Let's have a look." Coming over to where she sat, he settled down, crossing his long legs. He took the album from her and stared at the picture.

She scanned his face. His color looked a lot better than it did a couple of weeks ago, and the paralysis was barely noticeable.

"Espen was only a few months old, so that would have been at Havdal," he said. "We moved there not long before Espen was born. Well, Mama and Kai and I. Papa stayed behind. That was the time they split up for good."

"That can't have been an easy time."

"It wasn't."

She hesitated, unsure whether she ought to pry. "Would you mind telling me about it? I know so little about Espen's home life when he was a small child. I've asked Kai, but he doesn't remember much since he was quite young as well. I'd love to be able to fill in some gaps in my book."

"What do you want to know?"

"Everything, really."

He laughed, his smile full and unhindered by the Bell's Palsy. "Could you rephrase your question, please? I don't think that was quite broad enough."

She joined in his chuckle. "Just tell me whatever you think is relevant. What did your parents do for a living?"

He shifted the album on his knees. "Papa was a solicitor and Mama was a stay-at-home mother when we were little. I think we were comfortably off

while they were married, because I remember showing off new shoes and birthday presents in the schoolyard."

"And what was the general tone of your home? Was there lots of fun and laughter? Were your parents strict or permissive?"

His smile faded. "Before Mama and Papa split up, I remember a lot of yelling. Screaming matches where they'd get red in the face, shouting at each other while Kai and I ran upstairs and hid under the covers."

Bethany stared at him. Wow, that took a turn.

"At the time, I didn't know what it was about, but now I think it was because Mama found out he was cheating." He made a face. "It might have been because of me that she found out."

"How do you know that?"

"Papa took me to the dentist one afternoon. He got me out of school and after my appointment, we stopped at his office. He told me to wait in the waiting room while he went to grab something. I needed to go to the bathroom and when I went past his door, I saw him kissing another woman. Later that day, I mentioned it to Mama. She and Papa had a huge fight. She took me and Kai and moved out. It wasn't long before Espen was born."

"I'm so sorry," Bethany said. That had to have left a mark on his heart.

"We lived in a small house. Mama went from always being at home to working all the time. Our lifestyle changed a lot. No more big house and we had a tiny car that used to break down a lot. And although we never went hungry, there were far fewer treats than before. I'm not sure what was going on because Papa would have had to send her some kind of support. But we didn't see him for a long time after that."

He flipped through the pictures. "This was when we were living with our father."

Bethany frowned. "I thought you grew up with your mother when your parents split up."

"When I was around seven, Papa picked me up from school and took my brothers and me straight to the airport for a flight to Trondheim. My brothers and I went to stay with him from then on. We relocated 1,500 kilometers with no warning, leaving Mama behind. No one explained anything to us, and it's only later on that I pieced together what might have happened."

Bethany held her breath, hoping he would continue.

He rubbed the back of his neck. "When we lived with Mama, she sometimes left us home alone to go on errands. Looking back, it wasn't the smartest thing to do–I was only six or seven and she'd tell me to watch Kai and Espen. We were usually okay, and I was used to it. But once when she did that, Kai and I managed to lock ourselves outside the house while the baby was napping inside. Our neighbor saw us and called the police and child protection services. No one ever explained anything to us, but I can imagine how it played out. It was soon after that when we all went to live with Papa. By then, he had married the woman whom I saw him kissing in his office."

"What was that like?"

"Really hard for me, but Kai and Espen seemed okay."

The mention of her husband's name hit Bethany like a jolt. She was supposed to be researching his family background. But she was absorbed in learning how his older brother had coped. She hadn't turned on her recorder. Nor had she taken any notes. Should she ask Lukas to stop so she could get her recorder out? No, that felt like too much of an intrusion, like treading on a sacred space with mud-splattered boots. She'd never heard him talk so much about himself, and she didn't want him to stop.

Lukas said, "My stepmother loved Espen. He was a cute, bubbly toddler who never met a stranger. But I was a sullen kid who just wanted his mom, and I didn't understand why we couldn't go back home. We were in Trondheim for about nine years. Then my father died while on a camping trip with me and Kai." He paused, staring at the album. "You know, I think that's where Kai's troubles started. The camping trip was his idea, and he'd been begging Papa to go. He thought if he hadn't pestered Papa about the trip, the accident wouldn't have happened. Afterward, we all went back to Havdal to stay with our mother. And although that's what I'd wanted all along, I felt guilty because of how it happened."

Bethany's heart ached. "I'm so sorry for your loss. That's a lot of upheaval for young children."

"Probably. I always imagined Espen had it the easiest. He was younger and seemed to adapt to every change. Kai disappeared into books and his own imaginary world. No surprise he became an author."

"What about you?" Bethany asked. "How did you cope?"

He shrugged. "By being a good boy. Trying to give as little trouble as possible and keeping everyone together and in line. Moving back to Havdal was a big change from a city like Trondheim. I threw myself into the theater group and Kai was into writing and schoolwork. Espen was instantly one of the popular kids in school. You already know how he got his big break."

Espen. That's right. She'd started off wanting to learn as much as she could about Espen's childhood. But she was learning just as much about Lukas. They fell into silence, but it was a restful quiet, not the kind of awkward pause that screamed to be filled with words.

She flipped through several album pages. There were countless pictures of Espen. Her editor would be spoiled for choice. But not that many photos with Kai, and even fewer with Lukas.

Even in the pictures when he wasn't alone, Espen was the focus, as though whoever had taken the photos had wanted a snapshot of Espen and anyone else was just there as background. It hinted at a story Bethany knew too well, of the favored child of the family, the one around whom everything revolved.

She knew all about that. She was part of the background in most of her childhood photos, too.

She closed the last album and put it in the small pile she would show to her editor.

Chapter Fourteen

As Lukas hit the print button on his document, it dawned on him. He was feeling well. For the first time in weeks, exhaustion was not his constant companion. His facial paralysis was almost gone, and the aches in his body only bothered him when he was tired.

He had turned the corner with this Lyme disease, thank God, and maybe he'd escape the long-lasting symptoms his doctor had worried about.

Walking over to the printer, he extracted the freshly printed document.

Gunnar walked into the office, holding a thick folder. "Ready to do some work?"

Lukas held up his sheet of paper. "I've got my agenda right here. By the time we're done, we should have six months' worth of podcast episodes planned out."

"I've been compiling the exit surveys from the training weekend with Nordic Blue. I can't wait to talk about that." He settled into the chair in front of Lukas's desk. "I was able to glean some great content ideas from that as well."

"Ah yes, Nordic Blue." Lukas shot his friend a look. "They loved you so much that they want you to do their next team building summit and training session."

Gunnar grinned. "They did?"

"They did. And I hope you'll consider it. In fact, we need to have a talk about our next steps. I'm ready to end my sick leave, but I'd love to continue with our collaboration. I have way more clients than I can handle."

"And my podcast numbers are insane since you joined me on those last three episodes," Gunnar said. "I'm seeing an uptick in book and course sales. How about you?"

Lukas nodded. "Same here. I'm a bit pressed for time right now, but I'd like to talk some more about formalizing our arrangement. I don't know what that might look like, but let's block some time off on the calendar to talk about it."

"I'm completely up for that. Let's do it before I go back down to Trondheim. That'll be the day after tomorrow." He flipped through the pages of his planner. "What have you got tomorrow at two?"

Lukas opened his planner and agreed on a time to talk about their continued collaboration.

He closed the book. "Let's crack on with today's agenda."

Gunnar said, "Before we start, I think your PA mixed this up among the client files I was supposed to look at." Opening his folder, he pulled out an envelope and slid it over to Lukas.

"Sorry, I read it before I realized it was medical information."

Lukas stared at the envelope. The one with the letter from Drammen Hospital confirming Espen's vasectomy. "How did you get this?" His mind scrambled to put the pieces together. After he found the letter, he got out of the attic and put it in his pocket. No, he'd come to his office with it.

He slapped his forehead. "I put it on my desk and my PA must have put it among the files I wanted you to look over."

Gunnar nodded. "Oh, that explains it. I guess you'll want to pass it on to Bethany."

"No!" The word burst out of Lukas's mouth. Heat flooding his face, he stuffed the letter into his desk drawer.

Gunnar's eyebrows drew together. "Why not?"

"Because I don't think she knows about this. And I can't see what good would come out of dragging this out to light."

"I don't get it," Gunnar said. "Isn't it something she'd already know? And if not, isn't it something she should know?"

"Let's just drop it, okay? Let's talk about what we're supposed to be addressing. The first item on the agenda is Nordic Blue. Let's hear about your exit survey."

Gunnar stared at him for a long moment. "Okay. Some fascinating results came out of that." He opened his folder.

Lukas leaned back in his chair as Gunnar continued talking.

Gunnar was a smart guy whose judgment Lukas normally trusted. But in this case, his friend was off base. He couldn't tell Bethany about Espen's vasectomy.

She'd been so upset with all the things she'd learned lately about Espen. How would she take the news that he had taken active steps to avoid becoming a father? It was far better that he kept this information to himself.

He and Gunnar worked steadily through the meeting agenda. As they got to the second last item, he glanced at his watch. "We'd better end it here. Bethany's arriving with some decorators to get this place ready for her mother's party."

Gunnar shot him a look. "You and Bethany are hosting a party here?"

Heat blasted Lukas's face. "We're not hosting a party. Or, at least, I'm not. Her venue fell through and I said she could have the party here on Saturday."

Gunnar opened his mouth to speak, then closed it again, shaking his head. He stood and gathered his things. "See you soon."

Lukas watched his friend walk out. He could feel the waves of disapproval rolling off Gunnar. But Gunnar was wrong. He had to be.

Chapter Fifteen

ARTY GUESTS DRIFTED THROUGHOUT Lukas's house, circulating from the fairy lit marquee out in the backyard through to the dining room and living room.

Lukas went into his kitchen, weaving his way through the white and black clad catering staff. Bethany's party appeared to be going on well. He was camped out in his office, and the plan was to stay out of the way until the party was over, while still being

accessible in case anyone needed him as the owner of the house.

He grabbed a water bottle from the fridge and turned to go back to his office.

Bethany stood next to the kitchen island, deep in conversation with one of the caterers.

He lingered to look at her as she gestured to make a point. Her asymmetrical cobalt blue evening gown left one arm exposed, and the other covered in a sleeve of floating fabric.

She snagged his gaze and flashed him a smile. "Thanks once again for letting us use your place. And please help yourself to some of this food."

"I might take you up on that. I realized I forgot to organize a meal for myself."

Her eyebrows flew up. "You haven't eaten? In that case, if you don't mind waiting five minutes, I'll make you up a plate."

"Thanks. How's it all going?"

Two children, a boy and a girl, barreled through the kitchen, forcing Bethany to press herself against the wall. A server didn't get away in time, and the boy slammed into her, sending a tray of canapes flying through the air.

Bethany called after the boy. "Dag, slow down!"

The child paid no heed, running through to the living room.

She went over to the server. "I'm really sorry. Are you okay?"

"Yeah, I'm fine."

Bethany looked up at Lukas. "My niece and nephew. They're quite a handful. Here, let me help you." She and the server scooped up the scattered finger food, dumping it into the trash can.

Bethany rinsed off her hands and picked up an empty plate from the counter. "I haven't forgotten that you're standing there and starving."

"How's the party going?" Lukas asked.

"It seems to be going well." Bethany filled the plate with a selection of hors d'oeuvres and brought it over to

Lukas. "Mama's really loving it, from what I can see."

"Thanks." Lukas took the plate, popping a cocktail sausage into his mouth. The spicy flavor burst onto his tongue. It was so good to feel hungry again. Another sign that his health was back.

The head server came into the kitchen with two empty trays. He nodded at Bethany. "I think your mother's about to give her speech."

"Oh, right. Thanks. I'd better go." She threw Lukas a quick smile over her shoulder and walked out to the backyard.

Lukas followed slowly. He wasn't dressed for a party and wasn't even an invited guest, but he was curious to hear what Bethany's mother would say. The last time he'd heard her give a speech was at Espen and Bethany's wedding, and he'd got the impression she was a woman who liked the sound of her own voice.

The guests were all facing the marquee, where Bethany's adoptive mother, Astrid Tonneson, stood in front of a microphone. Statuesque with impeccably coiffed white hair, Astrid could have easily passed for a woman many years younger than seventy-five.

"Thank you all very much for coming. What a lovely surprise. It truly is wonderful to have reached such an age and to celebrate it with all my friends and family. Erik and Tina, why don't you come up here?"

Bethany's brother- and sister-in-law walked up to Astrid, their grins as wide as hers.

Circling each of them with an arm, Astrid pulled them close. "Thank you so much for organizing all this. I know it was your doing. And where are the children? Dag and Dora, where are you?"

Lukas looked around. His gaze snagged on Bethany. She stood at the corner of the tent, looking at her family, a trembling smile on her face.

The boisterous children joined their parents next to Astrid. Bethany's mother carried on her speech. Surely she'd thank Bethany next for all the work that had gone into organizing the party.

But the speech went on, and Astrid made no mention of her daughter. Finally, her son Erik stepped in front of the microphone and invited everyone to grab a glass and make a toast to the birthday girl.

This was ridiculous. Were none of them going to acknowledge Bethany? A waiter stopped in front of him with a tray of drinks, but Lukas declined a glass. His gaze slid to Bethany's face.

She still stood in her spot, eyes glistening as she accepted a glass. She raised it as her brother proposed a toast and all the guests drank to her mother's health.

The guests broke into applause, and the music started again.

Lukas couldn't believe what he'd just witnessed.

Head down, Bethany left her spot and walked toward the kitchen.

She turned toward the sound of shrieking children.

Lukas followed her gaze to where her nephew held a smaller boy pinned to the ground.

Bethany rushed over, grabbing her nephew's arm. "Dag, stop it."

The boy twisted around, grasping a fistful of Bethany's hair.

She pulled away, yelping as the hair came off.

Dag stared round-eyed at the wig in his hand, his head swiveling upward to look at his aunt's bald scalp.

Face crumpling, Bethany rushed past the children and disappeared into the house.

Chapter Sixteen

ETHANY HURTLED THROUGH THE kitchen and down the hallway, grabbing the first door handle that registered in her blurred vision. She pushed through into Lukas's office and slammed the door behind her, leaning her back against it.

Brilliant. Now everyone knew she was bald. She passed a hand over her scalp, her fingers making contact with patches of bare skin amid rough islands of buzz-cut hair. Her nylon wig cap had come off, too, so she was fully exposed. Hot tears burned her eyes. She slid onto the floor, face buried in her hands.

Someone tapped on the door.

"Bethany? Are you in there? It's Lukas."

She pressed her fists into her eyes. Why had he followed her? All she wanted to do was disappear and cry.

He knocked again. "Bethany? I brought your, um... your hair. I'll go away if you want, but I just need to know you're in there so I can leave this here for you."

Sighing, she got to her feet and opened the door.

Lukas stood with her wig in one hand. He held it out to her.

She took it, avoiding his gaze, and reached for the door handle.

"Are you okay?" He asked. "Ugh, sorry. Dumb question. Is there anything I can do to help? I can listen. Or shut up. Or go away. What do you need me to do?"

As his words tumbled out, something in his tone spoke to her. He wasn't just here to pry or gawk at her. He wanted to help.

She wrapped her arms around her body. "You could shut the door so I can have some privacy while I put this back on."

"Sure. Okay."

She stepped backward, and he followed her into his office, closing the door behind him.

The little nylon cap she wore to protect her scalp had come off with the wig and lay tucked inside. Her back toward Lukas, she set the close-fitting cap onto her head. Then, turning the wig in her hands, she found the tapering back section and slid it on. Years of practice made putting it on easy. She glanced at her reflection in a glass-fronted cabinet, combing her fingers through the wig's bangs. Her sleek pixie cut was back in place.

She faced Lukas, gesturing with her hands. "Ta da! Instant hair."

"It looks good." His gaze roved over her face. "But you look fine without it, too."

Bethany scoffed. "Yeah, right. It's kind of you to lie and try to make me feel better, though."

"I'm serious." He walked over to a chair and sat down. "Hair is overrated, anyway. The Rock does fine without any. Bruce Willis, too."

She couldn't hold back a laugh. "Those are men. Hairless women are a different story."

"I don't understand why it has to be like that."

She studied his face, searching for any trace of insincerity. If there was any, he hid it well. His body was angled forward, his gaze fixed on hers.

She sat in a chair opposite him. "Not everyone thinks the way you do. It bothered Espen a lot."

"When you met him did you... um, were you–" he gestured with his hand.

"Bald? No. I had a full head of hair back then. But a couple of years after we were married, I noticed clumps of it would come off in the shower and when I was brushing it. I'd find more strands than normal on my pillow in the morning." She glanced at Lukas. "Then Espen told me one day he could see my scalp. I went to a specialist who confirmed it was androgenetic alopecia. Irreversible and incurable, although they could slow it down a bit." She raised a hand to her head. "I shaved all the hair off when the bald patches became too big to hide. And I started wearing wigs."

Not just in public, but at home, ever since Espen had seen her shaved head. His look of disgust felt like her guts were being ripped out. She couldn't bear the thought of seeing that expression on his face again. And so, even with her husband, she'd kept her baldness hidden. No one but her closest friends knew, and nobody had seen her bare scalp. Until today's complete humiliation.

Lukas clasped his hands together. "Sorry if this is a dumb question. But andronetic—what did you say?"

"Androgenetic alopecia."

"Androgenetic alopecia. All it does is make you lose your hair?"

"Yes. It's what's commonly called male pattern baldness, which is weird because lots of women have it, too."

He nodded slowly. "So, it's not physically debilitating. You're otherwise healthy, and it's something many people go through."

Heat rushed to her face. "Are you saying I need to get a grip and not feel so sorry for myself?"

His gray eyes widened, and he threw up his hands, palms outward. "No. My goodness, no. That's not what I meant. I saw your face when your nephew pulled off your wig. From that, and from what you said, I can tell this is something that makes you feel a lot of pain and shame." He leaned forward. "But there's no need to carry any shame. Especially if it's rooted in any sort of belief that you're unattractive or… or undesirable because you don't have hair." Deep color flooded his face. "Even if you were as bald as Elmer Fudd, you're still beautiful. And not just on the outside."

His words flowed over her like a warm, sweet wave, soothing the chapped cracks in her heart. Her throat tightening, she turned her face away as a rush of tears filled her eyes.

His chair scraped back along the hardwood floor. "Sorry, I'm only making things worse. I'll give you some space now."

She looked up. He was already at the door. "No, wait."

He stopped, turning around slowly, his face red.

Bethany smiled. "Elmer Fudd, huh?"

His lips tipped upward. "Or Charlie Brown."

"I lean toward Captain Jean-Luc Picard."

He held up a finger. "If you're going into Star Trek, what about Lieutenant Ilia?"

"Lieutenant Ilia?" she said, frowning. "I don't know who that is. I'm clearly not as deep into Star Trek lore as you are."

"Look her up. Bald and absolutely stunning."

"Thank you. I will." She stood. "Thank you, Lukas."

His eyes warmed.

She sighed. "I'd better get back out there. I am supposed to be hosting a party, after all."

"True. Although from what your mother said, you had little to do with pulling this whole thing together."

She winced. So, he hadn't missed that, either. Her mother's speech had hurt. But as she looked at Lukas's face, the pain lost some of its sharpness. He thought she was beautiful. And, standing in his gaze, she felt beautiful. She held his words close, cuddling them to her heart like a hot water bottle on a freezing cold night.

Chapter Seventeen

HE SECONDS STRETCHED AS Lukas stared at Bethany. He couldn't look away.

She broke off eye contact first, brushing a finger against her upper cheek and glancing at the dark smear. "I'd better fix this mess before I show myself out there again."

She looked wonderful, even with stains around her eyes, but he supposed women didn't like their makeup smudged. He pointed to a door behind her. "I've got a little washroom cubicle over there."

"Thanks." She flashed him a smile and ducked into the bathroom.

He stood in the center of his office, irresolute. Should he wait here while she freshened up? That might look presumptuous. But he couldn't just go up to his room and leave her to finish off her hosting duties after her guests had witnessed the wig pulling incident. Nor after everything they'd just talked about. But what right did he have to hang around? He wasn't even officially invited to the party, although this was his house.

And yet one thought rose above the "ifs" and "buts" jostling for space in his mind. Bethany needed someone to be there for her as she closed up this rough evening. He wanted to be that person.

And so he lingered until she came out of the bathroom, her face washed and devoid of makeup.

Her lips curved upward as her gaze met his. "I'm ready to face the world."

He would clobber it and lay it at her feet if she wanted him to.

Hanging a few steps back, he followed her out of his office and into the kitchen, waiting in the doorway as she spoke to the head caterer.

She glanced at Lukas over her shoulder. "I'll do the rounds now and drop heavy hints for the guests to leave. It'll take the catering staff about an hour to pack everything up after everyone else has gone. Then you'll have your home to yourself once again."

"No hurry. They can take all the time they need." He walked up to the head caterer. "The food was delicious. I'd love your card, if you have one. Do you cater events in Havdal?"

The small, rotund man grinned, his head bobbing up and down. "Yes, we work all over East Finnmark. I have a card somewhere. Hold on." He reached under the counter for his bag, fished out a business card, and gave it to Lukas.

Bethany gestured toward the door that led to the backyard. "Shall we?"

Lukas headed out behind her as she made her way toward a group of guests standing on the edge of the lawn.

How did she manage to look so poised and serene after the way she'd fled from here earlier?

Lukas recognized Bethany's sister-in-law, Tina, among the group.

Tina faced Bethany, her mouth turned downward in a full-lipped pout. "Aw, here she is, poor thing. Are you all right, darling? None of us realized you wore a wig, and we were just saying how authentic it looks. To think I've always been envious of your amazing hair, and all along it's been a wig." She tilted her head to the side. "I really must apologize for little Dag. He's so high spirited and often lets a joke get too far."

"Apology accepted," Bethany said. She turned toward the other guests. "Thank you so much for coming tonight. Sorry about the last-minute change of venue." She waved a hand toward Lukas. "Mr. Meland was kind enough to let us use his home."

Tina's gaze flew to Lukas. "Mr. Meland? You're not related to Bethany's late husband?"

"He was my brother."

"Oh, I see." Tina's eyes narrowed. "Nice of you to step in and help Bethany in a pinch."

"She's family, and I'm glad to help." He looked at the other guests. "Thank you for coming."

Bethany's hand brushed against his arm. "I hope you all have a safe trip home. I'll take Lukas to say hi to Mama before she goes."

Lukas walked next to Bethany. "Nicely veiled hint about how it's time to leave."

She threw him a glance, her brown eyes twinkling. "Was it veiled? I was trying to be blunt but thought saying 'Go home now' might have been too on the nose."

A child's shriek pierced the air. Dag, the boy who'd pulled Bethany's wig off, was involved in a tug-of-war with a small girl over a stuffed penguin. The plush toy caught in the middle was in danger of being torn limb from limb.

Lukas twisted around to where Tina, Dag's mother, stood chatting with another woman. Neither of them took notice of the children hollering a few feet away.

Bethany hurried forward. "Dag, isn't that Silje's toy? Let her have it. Now."

"But I want it." Grunting with effort, Dag yanked the penguin toward him.

"It's mine!" Silje wailed, pulling back.

"Fine. You can have your stinky penguin." Smirking, Dag let the toy go.

Caught off balance, Silje stumbled backward and landed on her bottom.

Bethany wrapped her arms around the howling child. "It's okay, sweetie. You've got your toy now. Did you hurt yourself when you fell down?"

Lukas's gaze followed Dag as the boy sauntered toward Tina.

Bethany coaxed a smile from the little girl. She would have made an incredible mother if Espen hadn't stolen her chance. And she didn't even know it.

Her gaze met his over the child's head. "Thanks for waiting. Hold on a minute while I take Silje back to her mom. Come on, sweetheart."

The girl grabbed Bethany's hand, and they disappeared among the guests, who still stood under the marquee.

Bethany came back. "Where were we?"

"On our way to talk to your mother."

"Let's go." She slipped her hand into the crook of his elbow and his heart burst free from its tethers.

His years of iron self-discipline reining in his love for this woman were obliterated. And his heart rejoiced in its freedom to adore her without bounds. He could do that now without guilt, couldn't he? Now that Espen was no longer between them.

They walked toward her mother. Astrid Tonneson held court in the midst of a knot of guests. Her gaze flickered toward Bethany, but she continued with her lengthy anecdote.

Lukas waited on the edge of the group, Bethany at his side. She still held his arm, and he laid his other hand on top of hers.

At length, Astrid finished her monologue and turned toward

Bethany. "Ah, you're back. I heard you had a little mishap."

"Yes, but it's all right. I'd like you to meet my brother-in-law, Lukas. You might have met him at my wedding. This is his home."

Holding out a hand, Lukas summoned what he hoped was a polite smile as Astrid's pale blue gaze surveyed him.

She took his hand in a firm grip. "Hello. You don't share much of a resemblance with your late brother."

"I'm told I take after my mother, but he looked more like our father. It's good to meet you again. Many happy returns. I can't believe it's seventy-five."

She beamed at him. "Why, thank you. Clean living, exercise, and moderation work wonders."

"I was delighted to help when Bethany needed an urgent venue to have this party. She's worked really hard to pull this together."

Astrid's smile cooled. "Is that so?"

"Yes. She handled it all. The catering, the entertainment, the venue. She made it all happen."

Astrid rested a finger on her chin. "The one problem with surprise parties is the one being surprised can't give their input about what kind of party they want." She laughed, and it sounded like tinkling shards of ice. "I always imagined I'd have a nice sit-down meal in a restaurant for my seventy-fifth birthday. But I'm sure Bethany did her best."

Astrid turned from Lukas and her daughter. "Maria, darling, did I tell you who I bumped into last week? You'll never believe it. This is what happened–"

Bethany squeezed his arm, drawing him away.

Gritting his teeth, he walked with her to a corner of the backyard where burnished steel planters held dark green shrubbery. "So, that's your mother."

She looked up at him. "That's my mother."

"Why does she treat you like that?"

She let go of his arm. "Like what?"

He stared at her for a long moment, willing his clenched fists to relax.

She looked down, hugging her body with her arms. "Tell me what you noticed tonight."

He had to exercise self-control before he opened his mouth. To buy some time and school his tongue, he walked over to a low brick ornamental wall, lowering himself onto it. *Lord, please help me answer with truth and grace.*

She sat next to him, raising her gaze to his face.

"You asked what I noticed tonight," he said. "I noticed your mother was delighted with her surprise party when she thought your brother and his wife were behind it. She fussed over them and their children and didn't mention you once. Then when I said you'd done all the work, she found all sorts of faults with it. She criticized your choice of venue and how it was a cocktail party instead of a sitdown dinner. It was a wonderful party when she thought your brother and Tina planned it. But when your role became clear, she began pointing out the things she didn't like."

Bethany grimaced. "And you call me the blunt one."

"It fits a pattern I know all too well. Let me guess, and you can stop me at any point I get wrong." Leaning forward, he rested his elbows on his knees and his chin on his steepled fingers. "Your brother gets a pass on things you could never get away with. His every minor achievement is heralded from the rooftops while your significant ones are met with a shrug and a 'meh, I guess that's okay.' When you make the smallest mistake, you're shamed about it and never allowed to forget it. But when he makes really big blunders, they're brushed under the rug as if they never happened."

Her hands lay clasped in her lap.

"You didn't stop me," he said.

"That's because you're spot on. It's as if you've been a fly on the wall."

He shrugged. "Like I said, I recognize the pattern. It looks like a classic scapegoat and golden child dynamic. And my guess is it's been that way for a long time."

"You know I'm adopted, right?"

He grinned. "Yes, I know. The fact that you and the rest of your family are different races is a complete giveaway."

She smiled back. "I thought I'd mention it just in case you hadn't noticed. I was four or five when Mama adopted me from Ethiopia. She thought she couldn't have children of her own. Anyway, she brought me over to Norway. Changed my name and everything."

"Changed your name?"

"Yes. My name wasn't Bethany. It was something else that Mama couldn't pronounce. Hang on a minute."

She fished inside her purse for her wallet, extracting a small piece of folded paper. "I found it on an official-looking document from Ethiopia when I was snooping around once. It might have been my birth or adoption certificate or something. I figured out this must have been my name, and I copied it down." She held the paper out to Lukas.

He took it from her fingers, carefully unfolding it. The paper, torn from a lined notebook, was so old it felt like cotton, and it was frayed along its folds. Two words were written on it in round childish handwriting.

Berhane Gebre'elwa

He attempted to form his lips around the letters.

Bethany chuckled. "You're trying to say it? When I asked Mama about it, she said it was 'unpronounceable babble' and that's why she called me 'Bethany Gerda' instead. Of course, Bethany isn't exactly Norwegian, either, but I guess she wanted to keep the foreign flavor."

He gave the paper back to her. "So, you've kept this all that time?"

"I carry it everywhere." She slipped it back into her wallet. "I keep thinking one day I'll find someone who can actually tell me what it's supposed to sound like, because I've forgotten how to say it."

She blinked quickly. "Anyway, like I said, Mama thought she couldn't have children. Then she had her miracle baby when I was ten. Mama was never the warm, nurturing type to me. But with Erik, it was different."

"Because he was her biological son?"

"Possibly. Maybe it's natural for people to love their own child more than an adopted one. I haven't had either experience, so I can't judge her for it. Or maybe it was something to do with me."

He pushed a hand into his hair. "That's just wrong."

"Maybe. But I owe her. Remember in the mid-eighties when the world took notice of the famine in Ethiopia? She used to call me to watch whenever the pictures came on TV. She'd tell me if it wasn't for her, I'd be one of those

starving children with flies crawling all over their faces."

Heat pulsed through Lukas's body. "And so she's allowed to treat you like a second-class citizen because she adopted you?"

"I won't lie. I'm used to it, but it hurts when she does things like what she did tonight. The stories I could tell." Her thin smile didn't reach her eyes. "But I can't change her. The only thing I can change is how I react to her. And it does help me to consciously be thankful for the choice she made to adopt me and give me the life I had."

He stared at her, shaking his head. "You have way more grace than I do."

"I don't know whether it's grace or just me taking the easy way and avoiding confrontation. I really struggle with that." She sighed. "Maybe I'm deluding myself and avoiding dealing with things. But it does help to find something to be grateful for. I got into the habit of thanking God every day that Mama adopted me and gave me a home and provided for my physical needs. Without that habit, I don't think I'd have survived without turning to drink." Her attempt at a laugh sounded more like a sob.

His throat too thick for words, he brushed his hand against hers. She twined her fingers together with his, leaning her cheek on his shoulder. Melting inside, he held on to her hand, barely allowing himself to breathe as he prayed. *Lord, please allow me the right to love and protect this woman. Please.*

Chapter Eighteen

ETHANY'S PACE QUICKENED AS she walked to the entrance of her sister-in-law Lisa's home. She couldn't wait to see her friend.

Summer had long since faded into fall, and the lake reflected the yellow, brown, and deep red hues of the tree-less tundra landscape.

Lisa flung the front door open before Bethany had a chance to knock.

"Hi, sweetheart." Lisa wrapped her arms around Bethany.

Bethany squeezed her back. "It's so good to have you back home!"

"Thanks for coming early. It'll give us a chance to catch up before everyone else arrives." Lisa stepped aside, motioning Bethany to go past her into the hallway.

Bethany looked around. "Where's Bella?"

"Kai took her with him to walk the dog. He's got this baby shoulder carrier, and she absolutely loves it. There goes the timer. I'll take the rolls out of the oven."

Bethany sniffed the air. "It smells wonderful in here. What are you cooking?"

"Venison casserole and bread rolls."

"Yum. Can I help with anything?"

Lisa nodded toward the dining table. "You could get the dishes out and set six places."

"Who else is coming?"

Lisa slid on an oven mitt. "Sonia and Axel couldn't make it, but Lukas's friend Gunnar is in town, and I've asked Lukas to bring him. Johanna's coming, too. We'll use the blue and white bowls."

Bethany grabbed the crockery Lisa wanted and took it to the table.

Lisa pulled a tray of seeded rolls from the oven and set them on a cooling rack. "So, you and Lukas seem to have become quite friendly while Kai and I were away."

Bethany's face warmed. "We've had a chance to get to know each other better. You know how he's never really liked me in the past."

"Oh, he likes you." Lisa smirked.

Bethany's heart jolted. "What do you mean?"

"Has he asked you out?"

"No." She put the bowls down before she dropped them.

Lisa pulled a second tray of rolls out from the oven. "Would you like him to?"

"Lisa!"

"I'm just asking." She set the tray down and shrugged. "He's got some sterling qualities, and Kai and I were saying it's good the two of you are getting along better."

"So, you and Kai discuss my love life?"

Lisa held up a finger. "Aha. So, you do admit there's something going on."

Bethany looked away, recalling the long moment she'd sat next to Lukas at her mother's party, her head on his shoulder while he held her hand.

Lisa chuckled. "Don't worry, I won't put you on the spot. Sorry if I spoke prematurely. I just know what a solid guy he is. I'll shut my mouth now."

"Actually..." Bethany glanced at her friend. "I'm trying to figure out how I feel about him. He makes me feel safe. Grounded. Like he has my back. I'm not making sense, am I? I'll try to explain what I mean."

She told Lisa about her mother's birthday party, losing her wig, and the talk she'd had with Lukas. "With my

mother and even with Espen, I had to be on top of my game. Look my best, do my best. It was exhausting. Espen always liked me to look put together. I can't blame him for that. Men are visual, right? So, as his wife, it was my responsibility to look good for him. But Lukas is restful to be around. It's like he's the kind of person who'll see you at your worst and all he'll care about is whether you're okay and not how your condition makes him look bad."

Lisa wore a goofy smile. "That is the sweetest thing I've ever heard. And if you'll excuse me for contradicting you, I think you do know how you feel about him."

Bethany held up her hands. "Okay, okay, I admit that I like him. He stepped up for me when I really needed his help. And he's becoming a really good friend."

"Yes!" Lisa punched the air.

"But that's all there is. He hasn't asked me out or anything like that, and it's been months since we started working on my book revisions. The whole process has been harder than I expected. But I'm really grateful to have a friend around. You were away and Johanna's been all wrapped up in boyfriend drama."

Lisa rolled her eyes. "Don't get me started on Johanna's latest frog prince who's all amphibian and zero royalty. I asked her here tonight to get her mind off him. But what do you mean

about things being harder than you expected?"

"While doing research for my book, I learned some stuff about Espen. It's been hard. Made me question how well I really knew him."

"Oh?" Lisa folded her arms.

"You don't look very surprised."

Lisa shrugged. "You know he and I got off on the wrong foot and were never close. But I'm sorry if you found out some things that hurt you."

"I wouldn't say they hurt me. All of it happened before we met. It's just..." Bethany groped for the right words to express a thought she wasn't even sure she grasped. "I don't know. It was hard to hear how he treated people he used to be close to, and I wonder why

I didn't see it before. But never mind. He's gone and I can't change the past. And we did have a good marriage."

"So let's move on. Let's think about the future. And maybe Lukas is in it?"

Bethany laughed. "You are like a dog with a bone. As it happens, I'm going to Oslo next week for some publicity stuff related to my book. There'll be a special screening of Espen's last movie at the Odeon, followed by a gala dinner. I wanted to ask Lukas to be my plus one, but I don't know whether he'll come."

Lisa's eyes lit up. "That sounds lovely. I'm sure he'll agree to come."

"You think so? It's all the way in Oslo and there's not much notice."

"If I know Lukas the way I think I do, he'll move around anything that's not absolutely fixed and he'll be there."

Lisa's confidence sent a tingle up Bethany's spine. If Lukas liked her as much as Lisa thought...

The front door opened, and a voice called out. "We're home."

"Oh, Kai's back," Lisa said.

Ola, Kai's brown and white Halden hound scampered into the living room and made a beeline for Bethany.

She laughed at the dog's exuberant greeting and rubbed its silky ears. "Hi, little guy. Have a good walk? Hey, Kai. Aw, look at you both. That is the cutest thing ever."

Kai's daughter Bella sat in a baby carrier strapped to his shoulders. Her tawny cheeks were tinged pink from the crisp air. She squealed and bounced up and down when her gaze landed on her mother.

Lisa walked up to them. "I'll help get her down."

Bethany watched as Lisa and Kai navigated the safety straps and got Bella out. "Do you think she'll come to me?"

"I'm sure she will," Kai said. "But I'd better change her diaper first. Ola wasn't the only one who took care of business while we were out."

A lump rose in Bethany's throat as Kai carried Bella out of the room. His posture, his coloring–for a moment he

looked so much like Espen that she had a brief vision of what might have been if she'd been able to give her husband a child. Their baby would have had Bella's coloring, too, maybe with the same mop of silky brown hair.

Blinking quickly, she turned back to the table. "I didn't finish setting all the places, did I?"

Lisa was right. It was time to put aside the past with all its might-have-beens and think about the future. And perhaps another Meland brother would be a part of it.

Chapter Nineteen

UKAS PULLED HIS CAR up to Kai's cabin, his heart lurching as he saw Bethany's black Skoda already parked there.

Beside him, Gunnar whistled. "You weren't exaggerating. This place is breathtaking."

The men got out of the car, Gunnar taking a few steps toward the lake. Its mirror still surface reflected the snow-capped mountains and autumnal hues.

"It must be amazing to live out here," Gunnar said. "Imagine waking up to a view like this every day."

Lukas walked up to him. "It's spectacular, but a bit quiet for me. I like a bit of noise."

Gunnar laughed. "Which is why you live in the wild urban jungle of Berghaven. Population what, three thousand?"

"Three thousand and one if you decide to move up here. Have you made up your mind yet?"

"I'm still praying over it," Gunnar said. "But I'm leaning very strongly toward relocating. Especially if I could get a place like this."

"I hope I can convince you to stay. Let's go inside."

Kai opened the front door, surrounding his two guests in the fragrant aroma of home cooking. "Come on in, guys. Welcome to our home, Gunnar."

Lukas's gaze zeroed in on Bethany as she sat in the corner of the L-shaped sofa, her feet tucked underneath her.

She looked up at him, her smile shooting straight into his heart. "Long time no see."

"It's been a busy time even though Gunnar's sharing a lot of the load."

Kai took Gunnar off on the grand tour of the cabin and Lukas settled onto the sofa, glad to have a few moments with Bethany. He'd brought her something, and he hoped she'd like it.

"Did you make your deadline? I know how busy you've been."

"I did. Barely. With the new material, it ended up being more of a rewrite of the first half instead of just revisions. It's such a relief, but there's hardly any time to chill out. The marketing team has a bunch of stuff lined up." She bit her lower lip. "I actually wanted to ask you a favor, but it sounds like you're busy at work again and this is really short notice."

"Tell me what it is, and I'll see what I can do." He would find a way to help her, no matter what she asked.

"Okay, but please don't feel as though you have to say yes." She sat up straight. "Like I said, my publisher has arranged some promo events. Next week they want me to do the rounds of the breakfast TV shows in Oslo. And on Friday night there'll be a special screening of Espen's last movie and a big banquet afterward. I'm allowed to bring a guest, and I wondered whether you'd come."

Lukas mentally shoved aside all his plans for the next week. Gunnar would have to deal with the slack. "Of course I'll come. Friday, you said?"

She clasped her hands. "Wow, you can? Yes, Friday. It'll be a long day. I'll have to get up at, like, three in the morning to be live on Wake Up Norway, then I have another interview. The screening will be at eight, and dinner at half-past eleven."

"That is a long day. I'd be happy to come with you to the interviews, too. Give you moral support. You know how vicious you members of the press can be."

She chuckled. "Yes, and the real barracudas do breakfast TV. Are you sure you can make it?"

"Absolutely. Send me an email with the details and I'll have my PA book flights and accommodation."

"Thank you." She squeezed his arm.

"I, um... I actually got you something. A gift for finishing your book."

Her eyebrows flew up. "Really?"

He reached into his pocket for a small velvet box. "There you go." His heart pounded as she took it from his fingers. Would she like it?

She opened the box, revealing a thin gold necklace lying on dove gray satin. She ran her finger along the delicate chain. "It's beautiful. Does this pendant mean something?"

His heart warmed. "It's your name in Amharic script. Your birth name, I mean. I found an Etsy store that makes them. And, hang on."

Pulling out his smart phone, he tapped on its screen. "When I was on a work trip to Oslo last month, I met an Ethiopian lady. I told her what your name was, and she was kind enough to let me record her saying it. I'm texting you the audio file. So, now you'll know how to say your name, Berhane Gebre'elwa."

She looked up at him, her eyes glistening. "Thank you so much. I—"

Kai and Gunnar came back into the living room, cutting off Bethany's words. But she slipped her fingers into his and squeezed his hand tightly.

Johanna arrived a moment later, and Lisa called everyone to the table.

Lukas floated to his place. He had done it. He'd put aside his ambivalent feelings about his brother and helped Bethany with her book, and his reward was her friendship. Of all the people she could have asked to go with her to Oslo, she'd chosen him.

After the flurry and bustle of the book release, maybe Espen would finally remain in the past, his worst secrets buried along with him.

Lukas's new friendship with Bethany might not be much of a foundation, but it was something. Maybe, if he was patient, something more might come out of it. He'd already waited over twenty-five years for Bethany. He could wait a bit longer.

Lukas's heart swelled as he looked around the dinner table. Kai and Gunnar squabbled over the last helping of the stew, calling on Johanna to decide who deserved it more.

Bethany held Bella in her lap, entertaining the baby while Lisa finished her food. The child whimpered and

Bethany stood and walked toward the window, jiggling Bella on her hip.

Lukas followed her with his gaze.

Bethany lifted Bella in front of her, blowing a loud raspberry into the baby's round tummy. Bella squealed with laughter. Chuckling, Bethany repeated the maneuver.

Lukas grinned. When he turned back to the table, Gunnar's gaze was fixed on him.

Lisa stood, pulling the used crockery toward her. "If everyone's had enough, I'll make room for dessert."

Lukas held up his hand. "I'll take care of the cleanup. You and Kai just chill out."

"Thanks," Lisa said. "I'm not going to turn down an offer of help."

Gunnar got to his feet. "I'll help, too. It's the least I can do after denying Kai his fourth helping of stew."

"I'm glad to see you're not completely shameless," Kai said. "Your act of penance is accepted."

"I'll lend a hand," Johanna said as her phone buzzed. She snatched it up, frowning at the screen.

"Go ahead and take your call," Lukas said. "Gunnar and I have got this covered."

In the kitchen, Lukas scraped leftover scraps into the food waste bin while Gunnar ferried dishes from the dining table.

Gunnar looked across the cabin's open plan living area to where the women sat, Bethany still holding the baby. He slid a plate into the dishwasher. "So, you're going to Oslo with Bethany. Sounds like the two of you are getting closer."

"She's a good friend."

Gunnar was silent for a moment as he filled the dishwasher with used bowls. "Have you thought any more about telling her why she doesn't have a child of her own?"

Lukas's grip tightened around the spatula he held. "I've thought about it."

"And do you still think it's right to keep her in the dark?"

The two of them were out of earshot of the group in the living room, but Lukas lowered his voice as he faced Gunnar. "Bethany needs to move forward with her life. That information was confidential and only fell into our hands by accident. Espen is gone, and knowing about his vasectomy would only hurt her."

"I know it would hurt her. But do you have the right to keep it from her?"

"It's not about having the right to do anything," Lukas said. "It's about deciding when it's best to keep my mouth shut."

"Are you sure about that? I get that you want to protect her. But you're trying to control her access to information she has a right to know. I don't think that's a responsibility you need to be taking on yourself, and you're bordering on lying by omission."

Lukas shoved the dishwasher closed, rattling the crockery. "Would you rather I run around like the village gossip spilling all the juicy details?"

Gunnar's jaw tightened. "Come on, Lukas. You're too smart to rely on a straw man argument like that. And, I would have thought, you have too much integrity to try to justify what you're doing."

"So, you're questioning my integrity now?" Lukas fought to keep his voice down.

Gunnar raised his hand. "That was the wrong word to use. I'm questioning your judgment, though. Let's leave aside for a moment the rights and wrongs of not telling Bethany something so huge about her marriage. Secrets like this have a way of coming out. What if Bethany eventually finds out? Will you pretend you didn't know about it? How will she feel if she learns you were aware of it but chose not to tell her?"

Lukas attacked a stain on the kitchen counter. Why did Gunnar have to make so much sense? But the vasectomy information wouldn't come out. Apart from the medical people, he and Gunnar were the only people who knew about it. "She won't find out unless you or I tell her."

"I'm not close enough to her to tell her something like that." Gunnar crossed his arms. "Okay, suppose she stays clueless about that particular secret. Are there other things you're keeping from her that she's going to find out from somewhere else?"

Lukas straightened up, heat rushing up his neck.

Gunnar's stare was unrelenting. "There are other things, aren't there?"

Lukas turned away. "I think we're done here."

"Hey, man, listen." Gunnar touched his arm. "It's obvious that Bethany means a lot to you. If you're hoping to have any kind of future with her beyond just being friends, you'd better rethink whether it's wise to keep stuff from her."

Lukas faced his friend. "Look, I get that you mean well. But there's a lot you have no clue about. Can we drop this, once and for all?"

Gunnar held up both hands, palms outward. "Fine. I've said all I'm going to say. I'm going back to the living room."

He'd silenced his friend, but Lukas couldn't quell the uncomfortable questions Gunnar had raised.

Lukas had stood by as Bethany learned things about Espen's career. But that was nothing compared to the things she still didn't know about her late husband. Things that would have hurt her deeply if she'd known them while he was alive. And they still held the power to wound her.

Gunnar was wrong. Nothing good came out of telling people hurtful in-formation they didn't need to know. He'd blabbed to his mother about seeing his dad kissing another woman. Look where that had led.

And if he hadn't told his neighbor about him and his brother being home alone, she wouldn't have lost custody of them. And his father wouldn't have taken them on the camping trip that had cost him his life.

He'd failed his family by spilling secrets. But he'd protect Bethany by keeping his mouth shut.

Chapter Twenty

THE TV STATION'S FLOOR manager announced a commercial break, and Bethany exhaled. Her live interview was going better than she'd hoped. Sweat prickled on her forehead under the heated glare of the studio lamps.

The makeup lady dashed forward, dabbing at Bethany's forehead. The incandescent light was unforgiving, and Bethany knew the thick foundation was necessary to hide any blemishes from the TV cameras. But her skin felt weighed down as the makeup lady pressed yet more powder onto her face.

Emma Brandegg, host of the breakfast TV show Wake Up Norway, leaned forward and smiled at Bethany. "You're doing really well."

"Thank you." Bethany forced her shoulders to relax and shifted her position slightly on the pale pink sofa. The questions had been easy to handle so far.

She couldn't see the army of crew members who worked beyond the brightly lit set. But she knew Lukas was standing somewhere behind the cameras. He didn't need to get up at silly o'clock in order to attend this interview with her, but she was glad that he had. Knowing he was there made her feel grounded. She reached up to her neck, running her fingers along the gold pendant he'd given her.

The commercial break ended, and Emma beamed at one of the cameras. "Welcome back to Wake Up Norway. We're here this morning with Bethany Meland, widow of the actor Espen Meland. Bethany's written a biography of her husband that's going to hit bookstores in just over a month."

She turned to face another camera. "But Bethany's book isn't the only biography of Espen Meland coming out. Craig Carstone, the author of numerous celebrity biographies, has also written a book about Mr. Meland."

Bethany's blood turned to ice, freezing her heart.

Emma held up a hardcover book. "*Exposed* went on sale today, and it contains explosive allegations about Espen Meland's conduct with young women on the sets of his movies. Joining us from London are Craig Carstone and Annika Elberg. She's worked extensively with Mr. Meland and collaborated with Mr. Carstone on this book. I hope our regulars will excuse us as we switch to English for the rest of this interview. Hello Craig and Annika. Welcome to Wake Up Norway."

Bethany's heart roared back to life, pounding so hard that she could barely hear Emma speak. No one told her Craig or Annika were going to be on the show with her. And how had they managed to release their book before hers?

She wiped her damp palms against her skirt. She could get through this. She just needed to focus and hold her composure. The segment would be over in a few minutes.

On a large TV monitor, a lantern-jawed man with salt and pepper hair sat next to Annika. Her blond hair fell in waves that framed her oval face.

Staring at the gorgeous actress, Bethany felt every one of the ten years' age difference between them.

Emma set down the book. "Craig, let's begin with you. What prompted you to write this biography of Espen Meland?"

Craig spoke in a raspy baritone. "Delighted to be here, Emma. This has been a fascinating project to work on. I've always been fascinated by Espen's career. This is a kid who comes from nowhere with no theater background, no connections, and no showbiz parents pushing him, and becomes an A-list actor.

"And he's a non-native English speaker. Yes, we have guys like Arnold Schwarzenegger, Jean-Claude Van Damme, and Dolph Lundgren who've had successful Hollywood careers. But Espen was different. First of all, he wasn't a bodybuilder or martial arts star. He was a skilled character actor who spoke without a trace of an accent and went toe to toe with people whose mother tongue was English. Based on those facts alone, I thought this was a guy who has a story.

"Since his tragic passing, I felt as though no one had taken a really hard look at his life. So, I began asking questions, and it wasn't long until my path crossed with Annika's and the book started to take shape."

Emma nodded. "Annika, you contributed a lot to this book and, from what I read, this is primarily your story about your relationship with Espen. And one of the big revelations of this book is that you had a long-standing affair with him while he was already married, from the time you turned seventeen."

The room was spinning. Bethany gripped the side of the sofa so she wouldn't fall off. She stared at the screen, her gaze fixed on Annika. The woman was lying. She had to be.

"I first met Espen on the set of *Sunset at Dawn*." Annika brushed a strand of hair behind her ear. "I was fifteen and had a bit part. Although there was a spark, we didn't take it any further until a couple of years later when I had a role in *Mission Critical*. We saw a lot more of each other, and that's when the relationship became physical."

Bethany shook her head. Lies. All of it. Espen had laughed to her about young starlets who threw themselves at him, joking about how sick he was of all the unwanted attention. There was no way this could be true.

Emma held up the book. "And according to your account in this book, that encounter wasn't completely consensual."

"No, it wasn't," Annika said. "He didn't force me physically. But he was the lead actor, and he said he could make things happen for me in my career if I played my cards right. I was only a kid and star-struck."

Bethany's hands flew over her mouth.

Emma's gaze whipped toward Bethany. "Did you have any idea that this was going on?"

Bethany forced her trembling hands back into her lap. Her mouth felt like sandpaper. She shook her head. Her voice came out as a whisper. "No."

Emma turned toward a camera, flashing her teeth. "You're watching Wake Up Norway where we have surprise guests Craig Carstone and Annika Elberg live talking about the dynamite revelations in his new biography of Espen Meland. They're spilling all the details, face to face with Espen's widow Bethany Meland. We'll be back after this short break." Her grin settled into a smirk as she shuffled through her note cards.

Bethany balled her hands into fists. "Why didn't you tell me they were going to be here, too?"

Emma hid her smirk behind an expression of concern. "We only just found out their book was releasing early, and confirmed they'd be coming on air a couple of hours ago. We thought it would be great for our viewers."

A commotion broke out behind the camera. A voice shouted, "You can't go there. Can someone please stop him?"

Lukas strode onto the set, his gaze fixed on Bethany. "Are you okay? They had no right to bring those people on, and you don't have to sit here for this."

"Sir, you need to leave this set right now." A heavily muscled man loomed behind him.

The floor manager called out. "We're back live in sixty seconds."

Emma glared at Lukas. "Who are you? Security? Please get this man out of here."

"He's with me. I'm leaving, too." Bethany stood, grateful for Lukas's steady arm. She ripped the microphone off her lapel and dropped it in Emma's lap. "I won't be part of this."

Lukas wrapped an arm around Bethany's shoulder. He glared at Emma. "How dare you? Whatever Espen allegedly did, Bethany doesn't deserve any of this. You should be ashamed of yourself."

Emma stretched out a hand. "Bethany, please. We'll give you a few minutes to regain your composure and have your say."

"Thirty seconds," the floor manager yelled.

Clutching onto Lukas's arm, Bethany straightened her back. "I'll give you my say right now. I'm sorry for Annika if she was bullied into a relationship she didn't want. But what you've tried to do here, ambushing me like this, is a lowdown, disgusting ratings grab." She turned her face toward Lukas. "Please get me out of here."

Her legs were shaky as they walked away, but one thought dominated her mind. They would not see her cry.

Lukas shouldered his way past the production team and into the hallway.

They got to an elevator, and he jabbed at the button.

A woman ran down the hallway toward them.

Lukas stepped between her and Bethany. "What do you want?"

The woman, little more than a girl, gazed wide-eyed at Lukas. "Sir, I'm sorry. This is Mrs. Meland's purse. She left it behind."

Bethany looked up as Lukas took the bag.

The woman glanced at Bethany. "Sorry, ma'am." She spun around and headed back down the hallway.

The elevator doors slid open and Bethany stepped inside. Whatever threads of willpower and stubbornness had held her up suddenly snapped, and she sagged against Lukas as he folded her in his arms.

Chapter Twenty-One

WHITE HOT RAGE COURSED through Lukas as he held Bethany. Her body shook, and a dampness on his chest told him she must be crying. How dare they do this to her? All of them. Craig, Emma, the stupid TV network, Annika.

Okay, maybe Annika didn't carry as much blame. She was probably telling the truth about her relationship with Espen. It fit with his brother's typical pattern.

Espen liked them young. That was why Lukas had been so horrified all those years ago when Espen set his sights on Bethany. Lukas had felt protective of his sister-in-law Lisa's friend, then only eighteen. Although Espen wasn't much older than Bethany, he'd been far more jaded and worldly.

Espen had married Bethany, allowing Lukas to hope that his brother's intentions toward her were honorable.

But in the years that followed, Espen continued to pursue teenage girls. "I always make sure they're legal," he'd said to Lukas late one evening, wearing a smirk. "Not worth getting into trouble with the police with the underage ones. But as soon as they have that all-important birthday..."

Bethany stepped out of Lukas's arms. "Oh no, look at the mess I've made."

Lukas glanced down at his chest. Blotches of brown makeup stained his shirt. "Don't worry about it. Let's just get out of here. Wait, I forgot to push the elevator button."

He punched the ground floor button and turned to Bethany. "Are you all right?"

She nodded, sucking in a gulp of air. "I'll be okay. Thanks for having my back. For a while there I was just frozen, and I didn't know what to do."

"You were wonderful. I'm sure your publisher will understand that you couldn't stay. Those people lured you onto the show under false premises and then ambushed you."

Tears spilled onto her cheeks. "How could they tell those lies about Espen? They only dared do it because a dead person can't sue for defamation."

Lukas couldn't look her in the eye. He wasn't so sure Annika had been lying.

The elevator stopped on the ground floor, and he let Bethany get out first.

She dug into her bag and pulled out a tissue, which she used to dab her eyes. "I've got this interview at noon and then the movie showing and the dinner."

"Do you still want to go ahead with those?"

"No, if I'm honest. But I have to." Her eyes filled up. "I knew about Craig's book and that I'd eventually have to defend Espen against a bunch of vicious lies. I just didn't expect I'd have to do it today."

If his brother were alive and standing in front of him, Lukas would have throttled him for what he'd put Bethany through. She was prepared to go in front of the world and protect the honor of a man who had none, and to insist that her philandering husband had been faithful.

His conscience stabbed him like a searing hot poker. Was he going to stand silent and let her expose herself like that? If he allowed her to keep believing in Espen, that's exactly what he'd be doing.

He'd figure that out later. His first priority was to get her away from here.

He turned to her as they reached the lobby. "I'll call a cab to take you to your hotel."

She managed a small smile. "Thanks."

Fifteen minutes later, he walked her up to her hotel room, still wrestling with his dilemma. Bethany's next interview was coming in a few hours, and they would probably bring up the allegations in Craig's book. Was he going to let her face another camera and insist on her husband's integrity?

Her cellphone rang as she stepped through the door. Glancing at the screen, she said, "It's my publicist." She swiped her thumb across the screen. "Hello?"

Lukas followed Bethany into the hotel room, settling into an armchair.

With one hand on her hip, she pressed the phone against her ear. "I take it you saw everything as it went down. They set me up. They wanted the shock value of making me face my husband's alleged mistress on live television."

Lukas rubbed the back of his neck. *Lord, what shall I do? I'm not wise enough to know the right thing. Or strong enough to do it. Please help me.*

Pacing in front of the window, Bethany listened some more to the publicist on the line. "I would never have agreed to be on the show if I'd known they were going to stoop so low and peddle such lies. Do you think they'll ask about it at the interview today?"

For over a minute, Bethany listened, punctuating the silence with the occasional, "Okay. Yes, I see." Finally, she said, "That sounds like a reasonable plan. Listen, I'm going to put my phone on silent for a while. I just need space to think and pray. Thanks for calling. We'll talk later."

She swiped the touchscreen and sat heavily on the bed, dropping the phone beside her.

"What did your publicist have to say?" Lukas asked.

"She watched the whole interview and thinks it was outrageous. But she thinks a lot of viewers will feel the same way. Even if Wake Up Norway say they want to air different perspectives and give Craig a chance to talk about his book, they didn't have to go about it in such a sensationalist way. They meant to shock me by springing Craig and Annika like that."

Thumping her fists on the bed, she jumped to her feet. "The more I think about it, the angrier I get. I'll do the twelve o'clock interview and any other interview I can set up and tell the truth about Espen. It's even more important now that Craig's book is out."

She glanced at her watch. "It's just after seven. I need to get this muck off my face and prepare for the next interview. Shall we meet up here at five?"

Lukas nodded, his stomach in knots. He stood up to leave.

She touched his arm. "Thanks so much."

If he was going to tell her the truth about Espen, now was the time to do it. Before she did another interview. A verse from the Bible leaped into his heart. "Love does not rejoice in iniquity, but rejoices in the truth."

If he really loved her, he owed her the truth. Even though it hurt her, it was better than letting her believe in a lie.

He took a deep breath. "Bethany, there's something you need to know."

"What?"

He stared at her for a long moment, desperate to memorize her face before he shattered her trust in her husband, and maybe in him.

She let out a nervous chuckle. "You're scaring me. What is it?"

"I think Annika is telling the truth. What she said fits facts I already know about Espen's behavior."

"What?" Her eyes widened.

"He had affairs with other women. He told me about it."

She crossed her arms tightly as though she were trying to physically hold herself together. Her voice shook. "He told you? When? Who were these women? How long was this going on? Are we talking about a couple of one-night stands or something else?"

His words ripped him apart as they came out. "From the time you moved to LA, I know of at least two."

She squeezed her eyes shut, but a tear leaked onto her cheek.

Turning her back to him, she stepped toward the window and pressed her balled up fists against the glass.

He couldn't stand to see her in such pain. "I'm so sorry."

She drew herself upright, her back still toward him. "Okay. They threw themselves at him. They must have known how to push his buttons."

Bethany faced him, her eyes wide and dark. "It was probably my fault."

Chapter Twenty-Two

*L*UKAS'S FACE DRAINED OF color as Bethany's words hung between them.

His mouth worked for a moment before the sound finally came out. "You think his affairs are your fault?"

Bethany nodded, brushing away a tear. Espen was a visual man, but she'd let herself go, putting on all those extra pounds. Then her hair started falling out. No wonder he wasn't attracted to her anymore. And he was surrounded by stunning women who were star-struck by his fame.

Lukas's words intruded into her thoughts. "Why would you even think that?"

She should have known a woman like her couldn't hold on to Espen's interest. Her mother had made that clear when Bethany had told her family she was dating a famous actor.

She wrapped her arms around her body as a tidal wave of pain slammed into her.

Lukas took her by the shoulders, repeating his question. "Why would you ever think Espen's cheating is your fault?"

She looked into his gray eyes. "I mean, I get why he did it. A man needs to be attracted to his wife. There were so many gorgeous women throwing themselves at him, but I wasn't the girl he married. I already told you how he felt about my hair."

"But Espen loved to brag about how beautiful you are."

Her throat thickened, and she gasped out, "And as if that wasn't bad enough, I couldn't give him a child."

Lukas let go of her shoulders as though her touch burned his hands. He turned away from her, color flooding his face.

She sank onto the edge of the bed. Her infertility and fading looks weren't an excuse for Espen's infidelity. But they explained why. Any explanation, painful as it was, was better than the torture of not knowing why he'd done it.

Lukas came next to the bed, dropping to his knees so his face was level with hers. "It wasn't your fault. Espen didn't cheat on you because of your looks. He just liked sleeping around." He took her hands in his. "And he didn't cheat because you didn't have children. Bethany, he had a vasectomy. He made sure you couldn't have a child with him."

There was no air left in the room. She couldn't breathe. Lukas was still talking, but his words faded into the buzzing that filled her ears.

She whispered, "How did you know he had a v–a v–" The word choked in her throat.

His gray eyes were rimmed with red. "When you first said you wanted mementos, I had a quick look around the things in my attic. I found a letter from the hospital where he had it done. It was in the spring of 2002."

2002. What had she been doing in the spring of that year? Her mind was crawling at the speed of molasses.

2002. Her best friends had all come to visit her in LA. In the springtime. Espen hadn't been there. He was doing a charity event back home. Raising money for abandoned animals. And stealing her chance to have a child.

"Dear God," she whispered.

Lukas squeezed her hands. "I'm so sorry."

"Why didn't you tell me? I thought we were friends. And all this time I've been working on this book and you didn't say anything."

He dropped his gaze.

Pulling her hands out of his grasp, she jumped to her feet. "What else haven't you told me? Does he have a secret love child tucked away somewhere? Was he a wanted criminal? What else?" The last words came out in a shout.

His face ashen, Lukas stood slowly. He looked as though he had aged fifty years.

She stared at him, her heart threatening to bludgeon its way out of her chest. Why was he looking at her like that? There was something else. Dear Lord, she couldn't handle any more.

Chapter Twenty-Three

UKAS'S HEART SHATTERED AS Bethany backed away from him, her hands waving in front of her as though warding off a punch.

He had done this to her. If he had told her what he knew weeks ago, he could have softened the blow. But now, the weight of Espen's betrayal must have hit her like an avalanche. He'd kept these secrets in order to protect her from pain. But it had back-fired in the worst possible way.

Standing with her back against the window, she clasped her hands in front of her face. "I don't know if I can take any more, but I need to know. What else are you holding back?"

He pushed his hand through his hair. He had one last secret. His love for her. But how could he tell her that now? It would ruin whatever tiny chance he had of their friendship turning into something more.

Heat flushed his face as his conscience slapped that thought down. How dare he even contemplate about maneuvering to win her for himself? He'd blown his chance. He needed to do what was best for her, even if it meant losing her. And she had to know he wasn't holding any more secrets about her husband.

He swallowed. "There's one more thing. But it's not about Espen."

She lowered her hands.

Closing his eyes, he pulled in a deep breath and let it trickle out. "I shouldn't have kept all this from you. I thought I was protecting you, but it's only made things worse."

He took a step toward her. "I'm not hiding any more of Espen's secrets. But I have one of my own. I've been in love with you since we helped Kai and Lisa elope."

Her eyes widened as her hand flew up to her chest.

"I loved you before you chose Espen," he said. "And then I hated myself for coveting my brother's wife. That's why I didn't want to be around you. I knew how much you loved Espen and how his passing crushed you. And I was glad that his secrets were buried with him, so you would be spared the pain of ever finding them out."

She shook her head, her features crumpling.

But he plowed on. If he stopped now, he'd never get this out. "And then you asked me to help you with your book. When I found out about Espen's vasectomy, I thought the truth would hurt you too much if you knew it all. And I thought I could protect you by keeping the worst of it from you."

Groping for a chair, she lowered herself down. She hunched forward, her body curled in on itself, hands covering her face. "I don't know what to say."

Everything inside him wanted to hold her, to shield her from hurt and harm. But that was out of his hands. All he could do was wait and pray, and accept that he might never have the chance or the right to comfort her.

He stood rooted to the spot as time slowed down and lasted an eternity.

She looked up at him, her eyes glistening with tears. "What you just told me—I can't deal with that right now. I just... I can't."

He bowed his head, his hope crumbling to ashes.

"I'm sorry." Her voice was so quiet, he barely caught the words.

This soul-deep yearning for her... He'd lived with it for over twenty years. He knew every contour of the empty spaces in his heart. They would remain unfilled. But by God's grace, he would keep on keeping on.

He straightened his back. "You don't need to be sorry. I'm not asking anything from you. You don't owe me any response, okay? It's not your burden to bear."

She nodded, swiping at her tears with the heels of her palms.

He grabbed a box of tissues from an end table and set it in front of her. "There are practical things you need to handle right now. Is there anything

I can help you with? You have an interview coming up. Will you be able to go through with it?"

"I'll try." She dabbed at her eyes with a balled-up tissue. "I put my phone on silent, but I expect my publicist might want to get in touch with me."

"Okay. And what about the movie screening and the dinner? Are you going ahead with those?"

She massaged her temples. "I don't know. I need to think... to pray and figure out what to do."

"Can I pray with you?"

She looked at him, her eyes filling up again.

He read her answer in her face, even before she shook her head.

It was another punch to the gut. Praying with her was an act of friendship, of spiritual intimacy. He'd lost the right to do that.

Pouring every ounce of strength into keeping his pain out of his voice, he said, "I understand. I'll give you some space. Call me if you need anything."

She dropped her gaze to the floor.

He allowed himself one lingering look at her averted face before he left the room.

Chapter Twenty-Four

ETHANY WANTED TO CALL out to Lukas as his footsteps retreated toward the door. But her voice caught in her throat.

Her heart remembered the night of her mother's party, when he'd been her anchor. She wanted him to hold her and tell her everything would be okay.

But her anchor had flipped her world upside down. The past, as she'd known it, was a lie. She was lost and adrift, and the map she'd been relying on turned out to be wrong. And Lukas had let her live in an illusion, only coming clean when the mirage shattered.

Bethany sagged in her chair as the door clicked shut. She didn't try to stop the tears.

Espen had a vasectomy. All those years she longed for a child, measured month by month in bitter disappointment. He'd fed her hopes and watched her cry while all along knowing he'd robbed her of her dream. What kind of man did that to his wife?

Heat surged through her body and her racing heartbeat filled her ears. Grabbing a pillow off the bed, she buried her face in its cool, cotton softness. She unleashed a guttural scream from the depths of her soul. She yelled again, the pillow muffling her rage.

Throwing herself onto the bed, she cried and pounded the pillow until her fists were sore and her voice was hoarse.

She sat up. The pillow's pristine white was streaked with makeup.

Her heart jolted as she glanced at the bedside clock. How was it this late? She was supposed to be getting ready for her second interview of the day. An interview to promote her book about the man she'd once called her husband, a man she didn't truly know and who'd betrayed her and wounded her to the core.

She swung her legs off the bed, her foot brushing against the smooth surface of her phone. It lay face down on the floor. Its screen flashed as she picked it up. Ten missed calls. Someone was calling now, but the phone only lit up in silent mode. It was Lisa.

Bethany answered the call. "Hi."

"Sweetheart, I've been so worried about you. Are you okay?"

"I've been better."

"Kai and I saw the whole thing. I tried to call you, but it kept ringing out."

She rubbed the back of her neck. "Sorry, I put it on silent. I couldn't face talking to people."

"I'm glad I finally caught you. Lukas called and told us what happened. He told us everything."

Bethany choked up. "Everything?" Had Lukas given Lisa the full picture, or did he edit bits out, only telling her what he thought she needed to know?

"He told us about Espen's affairs and the vasectomy. I always knew he was a lowdown, lying jerk, but I had no idea."

"I wish I'd listened to you. You never liked him, did you?"

"No," Lisa said. "But he was smooth as silk, and you were really young, too. Who wouldn't get their head turned by a movie star? I'd give a lot to be wrong about him."

"Me, too."

"Lukas also said he's told you how he feels about you and he's not sure whether he's the person you need there with you right now."

Bethany's fist tightened. "He said that?"

"He asked whether I can come, because none of us think you should be on your own. So, I've booked a flight and I'll be arriving in Oslo tonight. Kai is on standby with his phone glued to his hand, so you can call him for anything while I'm in transit. Are you still going for all those events tonight?"

Bethany hadn't thought about the screening and the gala. She was supposed to go with Lukas, before the world had turned upside down. "I don't know yet."

"Anyway, hang in there. We're all praying, we all love you, and we'll figure all this out. I need to handle Bella now, but I'll call you. See you soon, sweetheart."

Bethany put the phone down. Lukas had made sure she wouldn't be alone. Even when he wasn't here, when she'd all but asked him to leave, he still had her back.

She touched her gold necklace. No one had ever given her a gift this thoughtful. She had a safe deposit box full of expensive but meaningless jewelry, trinkets Espen had wanted her to wear along with her red carpet designer gowns. The importance of each piece lay only in its price tag, as anonymous as its insurance valuation.

But this small pendant told her how Lukas had listened to her words and spent hours and effort tracking down a gift that spoke to her soul. And he hadn't expected anything back.

She picked up her phone again, ignoring the call alerts, and navigated to the messaging app where Lukas had sent her that sound file. She hit play on the clip, holding it up to her ear.

A woman's voice said, "Berhane Gebre'elwa." Bethany played it again and again.

Her mother had scrubbed out her name because she couldn't make the effort to learn how to pronounce it. But Lukas had found a way.

She'd been desperately grateful for the meager crumbs of love her husband and her mother had doled out to her. But Lukas constantly enveloped her with his compassion, sympathy... and love. Even when she hadn't realized it.

She hugged a pillow to her chest, rocking slowly back and forth, her thumb stroking her gold pendant.

Chapter Twenty-Five

LUKAS PACED HIS HOTEL room. Who else should he call? He'd spoken to Kai and Lisa, urging them to get down to Oslo and be with Bethany. He'd even called Johanna, in case Lisa wasn't able to come.

And he'd spoken to Gunnar. He didn't expect his friend to do anything for Bethany, of course, but he'd wanted to tell him he'd been right. Lukas shouldn't have kept Espen's betrayal a secret from her.

He'd wanted to protect her from the truth, but it had made a liar out of him. Thanks to his actions, the painful reality had landed on her in one concentrated blow.

He sat on the bed, burying his face in his hands. "God, please forgive me. Help Bethany through this. Give her strength to carry her through and heal her heart." His voice cracked.

There must be something more he could do. Had Lisa managed to get a flight?

Someone knocked on the door as Lukas reached for his phone. He opened the door and his heart skidded to a stop.

Bethany stood there.

She'd changed into a different out-fit, something yellow that made her skin glow. "Can I come in?"

He nodded, letting her walk past him.

She faced him, her hand stroking the gold pendant at her throat. It was her ring hand, but her fourth finger was bare. "You told me you wouldn't hold any more secrets back," she said.

"I won't."

"Okay. There's something I need to ask you about."

He stepped toward her. "I'll tell you everything I know."

"Espen once told me you refused to be his best man. Is that true?"

Heat seared his face. "Yes, it's true."

"Why?"

He swallowed. "I didn't want him to marry you."

She closed her eyes for a second, then turned her gaze back on him. "Why not?"

He scrubbed his hand across his mouth. "I wish I could say I was being noble and didn't want you to marry a guy I knew would hurt you. But at that moment, it was just because I wanted you for myself. I was upset that you'd chosen him. I almost didn't come to the wedding at all, but I knew I'd regret it. So, I came, but I hung around the back and didn't get involved."

"Thanks for telling me." She folded her arms and walked toward the window. "I'm going to the gala tonight."

"You are?"

She faced him, her arms still crossed. "I have a commitment to my publisher, and I want to do my best for the book. Espen had a lot of fans who want to know about his life, and there are other people in there whose stories need to be told. Like Morten. Will you come with me?"

"Of course I will. I'm glad you want me there." His voice failed him and he turned away from her, blinking away the moisture in his eyes.

"I want you there. My feelings about Espen are really complicated and messy right now. I'm in pieces. I'm trying to figure out how to go forward with what's left of me. I don't know whether it's fair to you to involve you in this kind of mess."

He spun around to face her. "I'm already involved."

"But is it fair?"

"I'll worry about whether it's fair. I'm here for you, Bethany. In whichever way you want me. As your friend, as your brother, as your..." His voice thickened. "I love you. I'm not going to hide that. But if you don't want me that way, I can handle it. But I'll be whatever you need."

She held her palm over her chest. Her eyes filling, she whispered, "No one's ever told me that."

She came into his arms, nestling with her head against his chest.

His lips brushed the top of her head. "I mean it, Berhane. I'm here for you."

His heart drummed a thunderous, reckless rhythm. He was fully open to her, and he had no defenses left. He yearned for her to belong to him, but if she wasn't his, he'd let her go. Whatever happened, he'd never regret loving her.

Her arms tightened around him, and he held her closer.

Epilogue

One Month Later

GUNNAR RAPPED ON THE pane of Lukas's office door. "Package for you."

Lukas looked up from his proposal report, stretching his hand to receive the cardboard box from his friend. "What's this?" He ripped it open, pulling out a glossy hardcover book. A closeup of Espen's face dominated the front cover, piercing ice-blue eyes staring toward the camera.

"I see the book is out," Gunnar said.

"Yes. It's release day." Lukas turned it around in his hands.

"Let me have a look." Gunnar flipped through a few pages. "Hey, you're in the dedication."

Lukas glanced up. "What?"

"Look."

Lukas took the book, warmth radiating through his chest as he read the two-line dedication.

To Lukas

The one who knows my name.

"What does it mean?" Gunnar asked.

"It's private."

"Oh, I see how it is." Gunnar placed his fists on his hips, making a dramatic show of being offended. "Fine. I'll mind my own business. But remember whose advice you ignored that almost cost you your girl. Just saying." He tossed his words over his shoulder as he headed to his office across the hallway.

Lukas grinned, taking another look at the dedication. Bethany was a good writer, but this would probably be his favorite part of the book.

She was in Bergen for a book signing, but she'd be back tomorrow. With the book finally released, her promotion duties should ease up. Then hopefully they'd get to spend some time together and find out where their relationship was going.

He'd not exactly taken a step back, but left her space to do what she needed to do. He'd promised not to push her.

He got back into his work, losing himself in his task as the afternoon stretched into evening.

Footsteps sounded in the hallway, and suddenly Bethany stood in the doorway.

He got to his feet, sending a pencil clattering to the floor. "When did you get back? I thought you were in Bergen."

"I was. But I caught an earlier flight."

He pointed at the book. "Look what came in the mail."

She glanced at it. "You bought a copy?"

"I know the author."

She smiled, walking into the office.

"I saw the dedication," he said.

"Thank you. I wasn't expecting that."

She looked around the office. "I don't think I've been here since my mother's party."

"Has it been that long?"

"I know, right?

She stepped toward him, slipping her arms around him.

He inhaled slowly, savoring her fresh scent and the weight of her head against his chest.

"I was doing my book signing. There was a decent turnout, and I think they sold a lot of books and other merch. I took some selfies and chatted with some of Espen's fans. Everyone had a good time." Stepping back slightly, she looked into his eyes. "And when it was done, I realized it was my last promo event. It's all over. My research, my book, my life with Espen. All I've been focused on for the last several years. I asked myself, 'Why do I need to be here?' I just wanted to come home. To you. To the one who's been my anchor within this awful storm." Her hands slid up his chest, and she tilted her face upward.

His lips were on hers, electricity surging through his body. She was all soft sweetness, melting into him, flooding all his senses, exploding his brain.

She broke away with a shuddering gasp, clutching his shirt as his hand traced circles around her back.

She whispered, "I love you, Lukas."

His joy was so deep, it felt like pain.

"I love you, Berhane."

The End

Book 4 of Milla Holt's *Seasons of Faith* series is coming in 2023. Join Milla's mailing list to get a free story and to be the first to find out when her new books are on the way.

https://millaholt.com/grab-this-book-for-free/

About the Author

I write fiction that reflects my Christian faith. I love happy endings, heroes and heroines who discover sometimes hard but always vital truths, and stories that uplift and encourage.

My family and I live in the east of England where we enjoy rambling in the countryside, reading good books and making up silly lyrics to our favorite songs.

To learn about my other books, join my mailing list, and grab a free exclusive book, visit my website at www.millaholt.com

www.ingramcontent.com/pod-product-compliance
Lightning Source LLC
Chambersburg PA
CBHW030806200726
48285CB00015B/1543